The

BALLROOM

Also By Simon Sobo
Commodore
The Fear of Death
Recollections of a Troubled Soul of the 60's (due in 2021)
After Lisa (due 2022)

The
BALLROOM

a Novella

SIMON SOBO

Copyright © 2021 Simon Sobo.

All rights reserved. This book or any portion thereof may not be reproduced or used in any manner whatsoever without the express written permission of the publisher except for the use of brief quotations in a book review.

First printing, 2021.

My thanks to Sarina Waters, Michael Denneny, Victoria Lucas, Carol Edwards, and, as always Linda, my muse and best critic.

Chapter 1

When it opened, the Van Doren Hotel in Boston was like any other hotel Vincent Van Doren owned. It was built in 1846, the same year as the Van Doren in Philadelphia and one year before the Van Doren Hotel in Baltimore. It began life plush, profitable enough, and of no particular distinction. Then, during the 1850s, it became Van Doren's obsession. His hotel in Boston became the jewel in his crown.

The change began with an ordinary conversation at a family gathering honoring the soon- to-be married Ernest De Vries, Van Doren's nephew. They had been called together to meet Ernest's bride-to-be, Belle-Elyse (shortened to Belize) Moreau. As we will see, she had a huge impact on the hotel, especially the Clarkson Ballroom, but even before that, her entrance into the family was already stirring up controversy. She was to be the first member of the family who wasn't Dutch–French, no less.

Belize's position as family outcast was familiar to her. She was invariably out of the loop. She was born that way. At least that was the conclusion that her father, in Lyon, not infrequently came to. He sometimes doubted Belize was truly his. Belize wasn't sure, either. She knew her mother was not always faithful to her father. She asked her mother and was told her father was her true father, but her mother hesitated as she said it. Whatever the facts, by the age of fourteen the tension between Belize and her father had become so unbearable that she was forced to run away. Belize's mother gave her a hundred francs and she was off to Paris to live with her aunt Celeste, her mother's sister.

She stayed seven years. She was at an impressionable age and Paris astounded her. The result was that Belize became more of a Parisian than those born and bred there. She was ambitious from day one, and an unstinting competitor. If she saw a quality in Parisians that she liked, she made it her own and usually improved upon it. She liked style. There was no better teacher than Paris, and no better competitor than Belize.

Then she had to leave. The son of the owner of the store where she worked was coming on strong. In any case, she told herself that she had gotten everything she could from Paris, so not long after she turned twenty-one, she found a way to get to Montreal as a French tutor for the children of a wealthy Canadian. After a year with them, she moved on. She was soon working at two jobs, saving for a shop she hoped to open, a fabric store carrying materials from Paris. She was surprised by how few stores in Montreal carried the very nicest things Paris had to offer. Their idea of style was invariably three years after it was over. She knew she could do better. At least that's how her dreams went until she met Ernest De Vries, which put an end to her plan. It had served its purpose. Montreal had given her life a fresh new kick. She now expected Boston to do the same. She recognized in Ernest what she needed most: a person of parallel ambition, dissatisfied, and forever looking to get ahead.

Julia, Vincent Van Doren's wife of thirty years, disapproved of Belize's restlessness. She had not yet met her, only heard the gossip, and she usually ran her opinions by Vincent, especially before they turned out the oil lamp at night.

"Restlessness is a dangerous quality in a woman," she intoned.

"Not always," he replied.

"A woman who gets married and wants a family?"

"How do you know she wants a family?"

"Then why is she getting married?"

Case closed. Julia extinguished the lamp on her side and was soon sleeping soundly. Vincent, on the other hand, had a head full of questions. They were all about Belize. He was attracted to wandering spirits. His businesses had brought him to three continents, far beyond anything his family could imagine. He usually found family functions to be a waste of his time, but he was looking forward to this one. He fell asleep shortly after deciding he would get a haircut.

On the day of the get-together, Ernest's father stressed to the groom-to-be that he should approach his uncle Vincent when he seemed weary of conversation and had disposed of everyone else. At that point, Vincent would welcome him. They had always had a special relationship. Ernest was the firstborn in his generation, so as a baby he had been a big hit with his uncles and aunts. And Vincent, had been won over by his nephew for a number of years, really until Ernest became a teenager, after which Vincent found him not the least bit cute. Nevertheless, on the infrequent occasions when they did cross paths, there was still a certain chemistry between them.

When Ernest was very young, Vincent Van Doren was his hero. His uncle enjoyed playing that role. He knew he was the pride of the family, the one among them who had become rich. Not just very rich! One of the richest men in the world. It was also apparent that a number of the men had very complicated emotions about him. He was envied, resented, an object of fascination, someone to scrutinize for whatever comfort his faults might bring. He was not a person with whom to enjoy a relaxed, casual conversation.

As a child, Ernest was much easier. Ernest recognized wealth as a good thing from the time he was four, especially after he asked Santa Claus for an outrageous gift, a rocking horse that he had seen in a store window in Manhattan, and actually got it. He knew his parents could not afford it. Usually gifts were made at home so it must have come from Santa Claus. Somehow, in his mind, Santa Claus and Uncle Vincent were related. Perhaps Uncle Vincent had written Santa Claus a letter. He didn't figure it out until he was older and put two and two together. After that, when he needed it, Vincent would help him out. The job he now had at the Astoria Hotel was most likely initially given to him because he was Vincent Van Doren's nephew, but Ernest had also made his own way.

It had taken him eight years, but so far so good. He was working in Boston, in charge of the Astoria Hotel during the evening shift, a position that usually implied he would one day be the manager of the hotel. His uncle was resting by the fire. The time was ripe.

"Uncle Vincent. Don't get up."

Ernest sat down next to him.

"Nice fire."

Silently, they both admired it, listening to the crackling logs, a sound that was set off by the patter of rain outside.

"How is the Astoria Hotel doing?" Van Doren asked.

"A little slow. Not much going on in Boston right now."

"Nothing is going on in Boston? Or is there something wrong at the Astoria? Didn't you tell me the last time I saw you that the Astoria wasn't very busy?"

"Yes."

"So––what's the reason?"

"I'm not sure," Ernest replied, "but my theory is that the Astoria would do much better if it stood for something. Right now, people come to it because the sheets will be clean, the beds will be comfortable, and it is quiet."

"That is enough for me when I need a hotel."

"I know, but there are dozens of hotels like that. What I would really like to see is a hotel that generated a little excitement, like the hotels in New York."

"You mean clubs and restaurants? I don't know about Boston. The puritans still have a pretty tight grip. People go to bed by ten, except for the Irish. And they have no interest in a downtown hotel."

"Maybe, but I think even they could use a little more excitement."

Van Doren was always on the lookout for good investments. Making his money work hard for him was constantly in his thoughts. He had a lively mind, full of questions, and was always doubting half the things he was told. When he was a boy, many people found this irritating. He'd keep wanting to talk about issues when everyone decided a subject had already been settled. It was a bit of a joke among several of the uncles. This young kid didn't know when to stop. But, as annoying as his stubbornness was, after he was hugely successful, Vincent's persistence was admired.

Van Doren liked Ernest's idea about a hotel with a distinct personality. Before he thought it over, the words were out of his mouth. On the spot, he offered Ernest the job of running the Boston Van Doren.

"Really?"

"Yes. I need someone with fresh ideas."

"I'm flabbergasted. This is going beyond generosity."

"It has nothing to do with that. This is a business decision."

"Still..."

"If you don't think you are up to it, I can reconsider."

"When do I start?"

Van Doren smiled at his nephew's quick response. "Take your time. Get married first. Then we will announce your new job."

"Thank you, Uncle Vincent. This is a wonderful wedding gift."

"If you are going to work for me, no more 'Uncle Vincent.' Call me Vin."

"Okay."

"One other thing. Don't say anything about this to anyone."

"If that is the way you want it—"

Vincent interrupted Ernest, putting his hand on his shoulder with fatherly authority as he stood and left the room without looking back.

The speed with which his future had been altered left De Vries giddy, and at the same time he suddenly felt more mature. He had arrived where he had long sought to be. He had always told himself that he deserved to be there, and now it had happened.

Van Doren's offer to his nephew was completely out of character. No one could remember when he had done anything remotely like that before. He was rarely impulsive and hardly ever generous to his extended family. Hard experience had taught him that if he said yes to one, they would all line up outside his door. On the other hand, on more than one occasion he had thought his nephew was special.

But more than family consequences were involved. Once they heard about it, his hiring pissed off several of his own men. For one thing, he hadn't yet fired the current head of the hotel. No one even knew he had been dissatisfied. Frank Porter, in particular, was very unhappy. He had worked for Van Doren for a decade. It had long been assumed that he would be first in line to obtain the next available position as manager of one of the hotels. More than that, not just

Frank Porter but all of his lieutenants found Van Doren's interest in Ernest incomprehensible. Ernest was a stuffed shirt. People like him were the butt of half of Van Doren's jokes, Americans with English formality. He called them "future butlers." They couldn't fathom what Vincent saw in this man, nephew or not.

As it turned out, they were wrong and Van Doren proven right. For forty-five years, until he retired, Ernest ran the Boston Van Doren Hotel competently. He was so honest that after fifteen years, Van Doren did away with his usual spy planted in management. More to the point, the Boston hotel was more profitable than any of the other hotels.

Yet, the truth was, Vincent could not have predicted this kind of success when he made his offer. His instincts weren't *that* good. His pattern was to stick to his usual cast of co-conspirators, men whom he knew well enough to trust, or, at least, knew their weaknesses sufficiently to understand which areas he would have to keep an eye on. It took at least five to ten years for him to reach that level of confidence, but once he got there, the people he put in important positions got the job done. Yes, he had hunches, and sometimes made decisions on the basis of them, but not when it came to hiring people.

Frank Porter's surprise at Van Doren's sudden decision was nothing compared to Julia Van Doren's suspicions. She knew something had to be up. Indeed, even more than his men, Van Doren had his wife in mind when he asked Ernest not to mention his offer to anyone at the gathering. The problem was, Belize hadn't been warned, and she profusely thanked Mrs. Van Doren for the offer. Instantaneously, Julia understood the mystery of Ernest's appointment. Earlier in the evening, she had seen the way Vincent's eyes locked on Belize when she entered the room. It was a momentary glimpse, and when they formally met, he was proper, but she knew her husband well—sometimes, he admitted, better than he knew himself.

Later that night, as they were getting ready for bed, Julia tested her suspicions, casually remarking that Belize was beautiful. He answered with his lying voice, the relaxed, innocent tone that worked with other people but had the opposite effect on her. A single syllable spoken in that tone and she knew. He said he hadn't really noticed Belize. No further evidence needed. The explanation for the job offer was obviously Belize. Julia had never liked the idea of a Frenchwoman being brought into the family. Everyone knew about their loose morals and deviousness, none better than Julia Van Doren. Her distrust of hedonism had been finely tuned by generations of Dutch practicality.

The truth was the success of the Boston Van Doren had little to do with his nephew. He was honest and competent, but the explanation was Belize. Within a year after De Vries took over the hotel the gossip began. More and more things were not adding up. Vincent Van Doren was a hardheaded, cussing, tobacco- chewing man with a fondness for spittoons. He'd quit school at eleven, in part because his teacher treated him like the rest of his family, like he was a loser. There is no way Van Doren could tolerate that for more than a minute. He was constantly getting into fistfights with the other children when they teased him. In a classroom, where he could not simply leap up to maintain his family's honor, it is surprising that Van Doren lasted longer than the first day of school.

Later Van Doren claimed, he quit because he had learned what he needed to know. After he became wealthy, he used to brag that if he had learned what they teach you in school, he would not have had time to learn anything else. His decision had its drawbacks. He couldn't write a letter without misspelling several words, which left him susceptible to scorn. But that didn't matter. Long before, on his way up, Van Doren had hardened himself to those who assumed their superiority to him. That the old money in New York laughed at his crudeness, considering him half ape, increased his ability to outsmart them. Through cleverness he had become richer than any of them.

Still, the fact that he was a cut-to-the-bone, no-nonsense man made the attraction he had to his Boston hotel more puzzling. The Boston Van Doren had become nothing if not nonsense. It was no longer really a businessman's hotel, nor a resting place for travelers. There were too many personal touches, surprises residing in every nook and cranny. The word that comes to mind is *exquisite,* which is the same quality that described Belize after she had taken over the decoration of the hotel. Each year she grew lovelier and lovelier, as did the hotel.

In the spring and summer, Belize's flower arrangements were from another planet. Sharp, dramatically defined angles and subtle color contrasts framed a truly gorgeous selection of flowers. No one in Boston had seen anything quite like it, especially the Japanese influence. Like other Parisians, she had been caught up in *Japonisme* after Admiral Perry and the Americans had forced Japan to open up to the West. Except the French were Japan's prisoners. Parisians were totally enslaved by Japanese taste. Belize succumbed to the graceful lines, the simplicity. Her long fingers moved like a pianist's, quickly, deftly, with lightning decisions made by her practiced eye. She had learned this from a Japanese master she watched, with an open mouth, one evening in Paris. She asked if she could watch him prepare for the following day, when his arrangements would be sold. She did not understand a word of Japanese. It was the process she absorbed, the rhythm, the intense concentration, the speed of his decisions, but also the speed with which he scrapped an arrangement and began again. It either was or wasn't perfect. If not, it was discarded. This held true when Belize herself began flower arranging, when her experience was minimal, and results preliminary, but even more so years later, when thousands of arrangements had heightened her skills to a fine edge of proficiency. The rule remained the same, perfect or discarded. In small things, her universe could be defined. Arranging flowers can seem like a trivial pursuit, but not when it is elevated to the level of ikebana.

It was not only flowers. From morning to night, Belize walked through the hotel perfecting the placement of things, moving furniture, statues, vases, bringing items from one part of the hotel to the other, adoring something here, moving it there, looking from every vantage point. She was like an artist working on the composition of a painting, or, more to the point, working in the spirit of generations of Japanese gardeners tending the great gardens of Kyoto over the centuries, deliberating on every angle, every inch of the soil.

That same critical vision had been developed years before, and further refined every morning as she studied herself in the mirror at the start of her day. Her jet black hair and blue eyes caused others to gasp. It soothed Belize's self perception. One might assume that, given her beauty, hardly any effort was necessary. But on the contrary, her beauty was her leap-off point. How she constructed herself was at least as important as what had been given to her at birth. She knew what every young Parisian woman knows: A new look is the only way to command continuing interest, including her own. Style is everything, an automatic reflex among the young. Her hairstyle, her lip rouge, her eye makeup were always inspired by the latest Parisian fashions. She would then improve upon that.

She perpetually re-created herself, Parisian to the core. Its fine fashion was her base, the ground under her, solid, but she liked to then venture to the edge, defying the conventions of good taste, flirting with the unallowable, then leaping to success. Like the hotel, her appearance was a never-ending work in progress. End points were a trap, permanence the kiss of death. Good hair days, if they tempted you to stay there too long, could do you in. Same for the hotel—while her eyes often widened with recognition that, at last, everything was stunning, the next day she was bored by what she had done and at it again.

On Saturday nights, when her work was finished for the week, her visit to Chez Girard, the restaurant off the grand lobby, was her pièce de résistance. If you were to watch her walk across the lobby, from the De Vries family suite to the restaurant, it would bring the same wonderment as a coronation. Not the pomp and circumstance, but the electricity, the anticipation of what might happen next. Arriving at the restaurant, she was greeted by chef Girard at the door, as if she were entering his home. Every week he promised her an unforgettable meal, a promise that he, in fact, kept fulfilling, even if he had harbored doubts earlier in the day.

Diners could hear the food crackling, almost leaping into the air as he sautéed it. They could smell the spicy aromas. Like Belize, perfection was his perpetual goal, fully understanding it could never be reached. At best hints of it might materialize. That was enough.

With steam rising from the saucepans Chef Girard was in perpetual motion. Swiftly he would swirl the risotto, sauté the mushrooms, turn the flame down on the onion soup, tasting each as they got his attention, adding a little more rosemary, a touch of pepper, two pinches of salt, and a host of herbs from Provence as he had tasted them as a boy––and of course, the butter he had discovered from a farm just outside Boston. Chef Girard has risen to these heights because he knows when a dish is ready. His palate was a gift given to him by the gods. It guides him to that precise moment.

Chef Girard personally brought Belize her dinner. He would watch her as she took her first bite, almost moving his mouth together with hers. He was not satisfied by a polite thank-you. He needed to see the delight in her eyes, the discovery on her lips. And when he succeeded, it was as if nothing else mattered. She had that effect on people. His most magnificent creations invariably seemed to be born when he cooked for her.

Born by the challenge, she brings her magic throughout the hotel to pursue her enslavement by beauty. Belize has vast open space in the lobby to make it magnificent, like the visitor has arrived to somewhere important. The club room for men with its leather and deep dark wood makes men feel like men. The frilly tea room brings a relaxed propriety that ladies enjoy. Her intuitions instantly produce the quiet thrill her designs deliver. Floor after floor of the hotel, each different from the last, create a spirit of adventure. After years and years of success after success, in her mind, she is just getting started.

And then there was Belize's garden, down a pathway behind the hotel. She loved all flowers. She had a passion for roses. The variety—yellows and whites, pinks, crimson, orange-red, lavender red, wine red--there were too many reds to name them all. The tight petals of her favorite rose, climbing the chimney about to bloom, gave her the same thrill as its fully open flower, as did the variety of her favorite fluffy roses, still others frilly, the syrupy fragrances at one end of the spectrum, and, at the other end, light and sharply defined whiffs of a scent, like fresh powder.

With seemingly no end in sight, once finished on one garden she is soon imagining the next. She travels beyond

Boston to wherever she needs to go, searching for a rosebush still more beautiful than the last one that she planted. In June, she couldn't wait for the first flower to arrive and thrill her. And when she wasn't thrilled, she wasn't capable of being sentimental. She knew what to do. In October, she tore out one bush after another. Some of the rose bushes were very nice, but not nice enough. Animated by her passion for the extraordinary, a very nice rose was just that. Very nice. There was nothing wrong with it. It just wasn't extraordinary.

She nurtured her favorites as if they were her children. Her youngest daughter, Ariana, loved roses as much as her mother and, beginning as a little girl, often worked with her in the garden. Some of these very bushes are now 150 years old. Belize would be very excited if she could see them today, especially Glorious Belize, a dark pinkish climber, which still grows on an archway above a stone bench. It was named in honor of her glorious beauty by a Sudbury, Massachusetts, grower, Julius Casanavius, as a sixty-fifth birthday present for her. He was one of many merchants half in love with her. Julius told her that the color of this rose matched her flushed cheeks as she warmed by the fire. This was after Ernest had passed away.

Given a vase, Belize's flower arrangements were breathtaking. She had a talent, but more important, inspiration. Some flowers enthralled her, demanding her worship. Her prayers were out of her control. She literally glowed. The flowers' radiance entered her bloodstream, saturating every pore. Her lips would form a certain smile, mouth half open, always with a hint of sadness, which intensified her smile's poignancy. Perhaps it is because perfection is made notable by its very transience. Sometimes a flower's glory can be measured in hours. Sometimes, in minutes. When she finished an arrangement, her eyes would water, more than once she was overcome. The beauty was too fine. Sometimes this would happen in the middle of her work and she could not continue. Especially in June, the bride' month, the rose's month, this might happen over and over, one rose after another.

In a woman of lesser beauty, her moments might have seemed precious, a conceit, unearned glory. But with Belize it all seemed quite natural. She had that star quality that comes easily to some and must be worked at for others to get there. When it's there it seems natural because it is. Others felt privileged to share her inspiration. When her gardener, Rafael, came upon a rose he thought might arouse her, it would stir him. For when she was transported by a flower, she took along anyone who was near her. Some say that her daughter Ariana's beatific smile was the result of being so often around her mother, when she visited celestial heights. They were probably right. There was something very different about her.

Most momentous of all there was a spectacular cut leaf maple directly behind the hotel which could be viewed from the Clarkson. Many have said that the secret of the Clarkson's charm is that very tree. It was rumored to have been brought to the hotel from Japan. Impossible, critics claimed, but there it was, and is, and how else can it be explained. England had started importing cut leafs in 1834, but they were saplings, meaning this one must have come from somewhere else, presumably Japan itself. No one knows how Belize could have found it let alone brought it to the hotel, but there it was, and is, in so many peoples' memory.

Belize had never before seen a more spectacular tree, nor had anyone else– twenty five feet in height, thirty five feet at its widest diameter, a four foot base trunk, every inch of every branch carefully pruned like a bonsai. Belize herself would climb a ladder all around it to maintain its elegance. Even in her seventies she would not trust her fine staff of gardeners to attempt what she was able to maintain.

The Van Doren Hotel would have made perfect sense in Paris. Or heaven. It was the last thing you might expect from a hotel in downtown Boston.

Vincent Van Doren visited the hotel repeatedly, presumably as its overseer, but it was obvious to anyone who knew him that his behavior had nothing to do with supervision. Like everyone else, he was completely won over by the place. At first horrified by the cost of the maple, Van Doren later took great pride that he owned it. He had never been associated with the smart crowd, never went to their hotspots and certainly never before had owned a place where they liked to congregate. He was not a parlor gentleman. In his hometown, New York society found him vulgar, even comical. Before he gave up on them, his origins were accentuated the harder he tried to impress them. His background disqualified him from serious respect in

Boston also, but with the exception of a few of Belize's enemies, the hotel was so charming, unchallenged as the place to be, that Vincent Van Doren was incidental.

Chapter 2

Vincent Van Doren came from his own world, a very typical one at the time. He was born to a poor farming family in 1798. Like everyone else the Van Dorens were barely getting by. A bad harvest and they could starve the following winter. They shared the same heritage as their neighbors. His great-grandfather, like half of all those who emigrated to America, came as an indentured servant, literally a slave for a specified period of time.

The family stories had been repeated so often that they had an important impact on everyone in the family. The first question was, why would anyone agree to be a slave? Especially today we are so comfortable that it's hard to imagine the desperation that characterized their lives. The average person, if they reached twenty, wasn't expected to make it much beyond forty. Peasants in the Netherlands, and elsewhere in Europe, sometimes sold their children into servitude, or they sold themselves for more than the usual number of years to pay for passage across the sea. That was the case for the Van Dorens. They knew what they were getting into, but after two very difficult winters, they felt they had little choice––America or die of starvation.

The passage was a chapter in itself. They were packed densely, like herring, in the sea vessel—four to six hundred souls, each receiving a place scarcely two feet wide and six feet long in the bedstead. There was constant misery. Stench, fumes, vomiting, fever, dysentery, headache, heat, constipation, diarrhea, boils, scurvy, mouth rot, and the like, all of which they were sure came from the old and sharply salted meat and other food, not to mention bad and foul water. Many died miserably.

Although the usual arrangement was four to seven years of servitude, if a spouse died on the voyage, the husband or wife who survived could be liable for eight to fourteen years. Vincent's great-grandfather's wife became pregnant, which led their owner to whip her. He demanded an extra year. Indentured servants could be whipped as their owner saw fit. Or, if an owner felt they hadn't worked hard enough, they could be credited with a half of day's work in fulfillment of their debt, or none at all.

The whipping of his wife led to their decision to escape, an unfortunate choice. Remaining in servitude was a contracted agreement. It was the law of the land. Rewards were posted. Escapees were hunted down by sheriffs and brought before a judge. They were uncaptured for less than two days. The verdict resulted in further lashings, and in their case a two-year extension of their contract. Plus permanently being chained at night using an iron collar.

So, compared to their forefathers, and people still coming from the Netherlands, when Vincent was born, the Van Doren family had already moved ahead, above the most important rung on the ladder. They were free. They could not be made miserable because of the whims of their owners. They had to do that for themselves. (And Vincent's father had a talent for doing that). Even if he hadn't, from a more modern vantage point, despite generations of effort, they like most farmers, had hardly gotten anywhere. They didn't own the land they worked. Today, we think of the average family as middle-class. Most people are so comfortable that only in their nightmares, or in movies or TV shows, does horror enter their experience. We are able to remind ourselves, just as we remind our children, that it is only make-believe.

The only reminder available to those bearing the misfortunes of the eighteenth century was God and the possibility of an afterlife. Prayers were as fervent as the workout many Americans today subject themselves to. Pray they had to do. In seventeenth-century New England, about 40 percent of the population died before reaching adulthood. It gradually got better, but still in 1796, four out of every five Americans were farmers—-meaning they were eking out survival from the land. They were completely familiar with desperation.

The Van Dorens might have a good year, and at one point five good years, but when their crops failed in the fall of 1806, they were in serious trouble. Years before as a result of a foolish investment, Vincent's father had lost one of the family's two cows. That year, their remaining cow died, so there was no milk. They had never seen their way clear to afford very many pigs and chickens. During that winter, Vincent and his siblings ate nothing but potatoes, and not enough of them to stifle their hunger completely. Once or twice, Vincent and his siblings ate paper. It was that very winter that Vincent's older brother died. They weren't able to keep the house warm.

Vincent's father was illiterate. His father's parents had both died when he was six and so he was raised by a cousin, who wanted to get the most work out of him that he could. That meant the cousin wasn't willing to let Vincent's father go to school. To make things worse, his father was a dreamer. As with the cow, whenever it seemed the Van Dorens might be getting ahead, he'd blow it all on one cockeyed scheme after another.

His mother also came from unfortunate circumstance. After her father died, she and her four siblings were parceled out to those who would raise them, so that they wouldn't starve. Vincent's mother was more fortunate then some of the others. She was raised by a kind parson who had known her father. She was the servant to his family, but he taught her to read and write.

His mother's sister married well. The land the Van Dorens now farmed was owned by her sister's husband, who worked the adjacent farm. Julia was his aunt's oldest daughter. As cousins Vincent and Julia knew each other from an early age. They were born the same year, but for the most part, they ignored each other until their adolescence, when their hormones kicked in. At that point, they could not get enough of each other. They spent long, happy hours lying beneath a giant oak, kissing and finally exploring each other's bodies. Afterward, they talked about their future.

No one was disturbed by their infatuation. Marrying a first cousin was common. In many ways, it was preferred. Rather a known family member than bringing a stranger into the fold. Vincent and Julia agreed that they didn't want to live the life of a farmer. At that point neither anticipated the low regard they would be held in by the upper crust of society. Neither expected to be among them.

As a boy, Vincent suffered from his family's low position in the community. His father was seen as a fool, and so Vincent, even after he quit school, when he was eleven or twelve, continued to be mocked by many of the other boys. While he got in a lot of fights, fortuitously, he grew big and tall and eventually won all of them. His fierce competitiveness and physical strength remained with him all his life. Indeed, well into his forties, he still got into fistfights, as insults continued.

He had an additional benefit. Vincent was inspired by his mother's unconquerable pride. True, she had been raised as a servant, but his mother happily remembered her father before he died. In good part, her admiration for him was helped by the parson's respect for her father. It wasn't so much anecdotes he told her as the tone of his voice when he spoke of him. That planted the seed and she took it from there. Her father grew and grew in stature. It was this grandfather who formed the basis of who Vincent intended to be.

Not that he was completely different from his father. Like many in similar circumstances, having creative dreams was the only way out. But the problem with many of his father's projects was that he gave up too quickly. After a burst of energy, he invariably became convinced that his plans were futile. Vincent never gave up on anything he started.

Julia was three months pregnant when they married. He got a job on a steamship that went from Manhattan to Philadelphia, stopping overnight in New Brunswick, New Jersey. Vincent had caught the imagination of Mr. Nivens, the owner of the steamship, who saw a little bit of himself in Vincent. With the birth of his son, Van Doren was told by Nivens that he had an empty waterside tavern in New Brunswick. It was in terrible shape, but if he was able to fix it up, Vincent could use the building for his family.

Julia looked over the main room of the dilapidated tavern. It was covered in moldy dust. The smell of cat piss and stale beer is overwhelming. Several feral cats sneak around. While holding the baby, she picks up some chairs lying on the floor and puts them upright. She tests each of them by sitting on them. They are sturdy. She picks up an oily rag to dispose of it. Her eyes are drawn to a decaying rat. A wave of nausea grabs hold of her. But that passes.

Her mother would be proud of her fortitude. She still remembers the two of them cleaning the pigsty when she was a young girl. She remembers squirming when the manure went over her shoes, touching her ankles. Seeing her reaction, her mother smiled ironically, and that seemed to feed her enthusiasm for their task. She doubled the energy she was putting into her shoveling. Inspired by her mother's example, soon Julia was doing the same.

There were many other occasions when they were surrounded by shit and kept focused on their task. Yes, Julia occasionally squawked, but she also eventually learned there was no point. A farm is a farm. The work never ends. Farm parents teach many lessons, but one of the most important is a positive value, pride when you get a task done.

Vincent gets a shovel and puts the rat in the refuse heap outside. She continues to survey the inn.

"It's big enough. That's the main thing."

The inn's possibilities are exactly what they had talked about when they were given the offer. She puts down her sleeping baby on a blanket she has brought, rolling up her sleeves, determined to set things right. Starting with a rusty pot and a broken chair, she takes them outside to add to the junkpile. She reaches for a glass on a shelf behind the bar. The entire shelf comes crashing down, dozens of glasses breaking. That deepens her resolve. After checking that her baby is all right, she carefully picks through the glasses, saving the unbroken ones.

Sucking on her finger, which is oozing blood from a small cut, she then goes from room to room, putting the unusable things in the center of each room. Finally, she returns to the original spot and turns to Vincent's pile. He had carried a broken end table to the heap. He examines a chair she had brought there.

"I can fix this."

She takes the chair and puts it back with the junk. He doesn't give her an argument. The longer they work, the inn's possibilities begin to be confirmed. The inn can hold a large family, which she intends to have. Moreover, it is large enough to house many paying guests.

She likes the idea of running the business herself. It means having her own money. She understands why Vincent is so tight with his money. Her father was the same, but Vincent takes it to extremes. Her father could occasionally loosen up and give her mother money for a treat, confections from the store, food not coming from the farm, clothing that they hadn't made for themselves.

Vincent won't spare a penny. He's obsessed with saving enough to start their business. Treats will only postpone their opportunity. She doesn't disagree when it comes to money, but she wants to have a say. Since he is the one who works to bring home the money, it is right for him to have the final word, but now she will have some money, and it makes a difference, even if she also saves every penny.

Working seven days a week is in their blood. Both families viewed daily life the same way. Work isn't something you choose. It is a never-ending given. It invents virtues other than satisfaction. It forms the dos and don'ts of your morality. Once you are no longer a child, it's understood that if you aren't working, you're shirking responsibilities.

On her hands and knees, again pregnant, Julia sticks her scrub brush in a soapy bucket. She mumbles at a floor stain, "Your days are numbered."

She doubles her elbow grease. Her smile widens as she looks for traces of the stain from every angle. She spots something. She returns to attack mode and it's soon gone. Not a trace is left. Contentedly, she spots another stain, kicks the bucket toward it.

The following day, Julia is buying rags from a rag cart. She puts together a pile that she likes. She haggles over the price with the merchant. He won't budge. She starts to walk away. The merchant comes after her.

Sitting by the fire late at night, the baby asleep, she sews the rags together into a bedspread. She finishes and starts another one. Vincent is doing his books by the candlelight. They are peaceful.

The next morning, admiring the finished bedspread, she sighs contentedly. It momentarily catches Vincent's attention, but he has other things on his mind—namely, what is ahead for him that day at work. She dusts off their Delft vase from their grandmother over the mantel in the dining room with a feather duster. It is their only valuable possession.

A week later, Vincent is on a ladder. Julia directs him where to place a sign reading, THE CLARKSON, over the front door. The decision made, he bangs in several nails. After he comes down from the ladder, they study the sign. She has worked hard prettying it up. They are both excited. They smile at each other, then look back up at the sign. Julia's eyes are open wide. The Clarkson was chosen as the name of the inn because that was the name of the richest family in town. Of English stock, Herbert and Elsa Clarkson were not necessarily loved, but they were respected by both of their parents. They are their only representation of class.

Weeks later, a steamship pulls up to the dock at New Brunswick. Vincent leads a contingent of fifteen passengers from the dock to the Clarkson.

In the dining room of the inn, guests are having dinner at a large dining room table. There is animated conversation. Julia brings in a large casserole. On Wednesday nights, she serves her mother's bahmi goreng. Friday, Vincent's mother's boerenkool is on the menu.

Bahmi on Wednesdays, boerenkool on Fridays––interestingly, both Vincent's mother and Aunt Beth learned how to make those dishes from Vincent's father. Without a mother, on his own, before he got married he taught himself. For whatever reason, he had a knack.

For the most part, even years later, Vincent and Julia Van Doren don't like to look back at their hungry years. But on the rare times they do, not when they are together, but alone with their thoughts in front of the fireplace. Truth is, if confronted, they could possibly admit that they were too caught up in bickering back then to remember nice things.

But for the most part, it wasn't nice. Van Doren's sin was that he was a better fighter than Julia. So, she was the one that landed up crying. There was virtue, however, in their business plan. They were able to save enough money during those ten years in New Brunswick to start an inn in New York, which became a hotel, and the rest is history–– during the next fifteen years, hotel after hotel in all of the major cities, then railroads, then ships. Vincent's big dreams consistently yielded fantastic results.

Chapter 3

The front of the menu in the Vincent Breakfast Parlor in 2021 states that the Van Doren Hotel was built on the exact spot that the original Boston Brahmins, families such as the Lowells, Cabots, and Lodges, first built their homes. The old families in Boston find this claim absurd. It is off by miles. Besides, the Cabots and Lowells would never have demolished their homesteads even for a fabulous price. They were not that easily bought off. A wit at the time described the Brahmins in this way: "And this is good old Boston . . . where the Lowells speak only to Cabots, and the Cabots speak only to God." Yes, the land was owned by the Cabot family. However, there the evidence ends. They owned land all over Boston. Their homes were not for sale. The Brahmins wanted nothing to do with Van Doren riffraff.

But the Brahmins' attitude didn't stop their children from attending the balls at the Clarkson Ballroom in the hotel. There was nothing they could do. While their decorum was perfectly suitable at home to conduct daily business, it was useless for a night of fun. The balls held at their homes were too proper. They were paltry imitations of something witnessed in England, a suffocating exercise totally without the spark that distinguished the Clarkson's occasions.

There, the goings-on were often uncouth, or downright rude, everything parents devoted themselves to eliminating in their children. But that was exactly the edge that made the Clarkson balls dazzling. The moment you stepped into the room, you could feel it, the musicians attacking their instruments with abandon, violins ringing out their melodies with a gusto that fed the gaiety of the dancers, who, in turn, brought the musicians to still another level.

Those on the dance floor knew they were at the cutting edge. When it became popular in America, the Viennese waltz was first named "the Boston" because it was first danced in 1834 in the Beacon Hill mansion of Mrs. Otis. They took it to still the next level at the Clarkson. Four different versions of the Boston were invented, not including the Boston Dip, which had first been created there, as well. The dip was executed with a huge step that would make the knees bend the body down. Partners held their hands on each other's hips.

"The devil's playground," Mrs. Otis's minister cried out during a sermon. "Make no mistake" he shouted. "The temptations offered by the devil are glorious, which is why they must be feared. They are the first step to sin." His sermons were very convincing, even to the children. But by Saturday night, last Sunday's morning sermons were long forgotten.

After all, what is wit compared to laughter? And oh, the laughter in the Clarkson. And, in the early days, the wrestling, the challenges to duels, sometimes shouting—almost every year there was some sort of fight. These were not affairs that could end in a whisper.

While some of the parents were confused by their children's refusal to be stopped from going to the Clarkson, the honest among them could take it in better stride than those with short memories. Yes, the possibility of bad blood mingling with their own couldn't be swept from the back of any of their minds. There had been, in fact, several instances of intermarriage between the classes. But they also remembered their own youth, the thrill of taking chances, that dizzying state where risk appears only as an afterthought. Most knew they could not stop this, the price too high if they succeeded. A child made overly serious and cautious too early, and too emphatically, will later miss the opportunities for pleasure never taken. And then watch out.

Young people's attraction to wildness is an elemental force, a given, like a hurricane or a flood. The lure of pleasure cannot be eliminated from their behavior. The dialectic continues in every generation. Indeed, no sooner were subsequent generations of the Van Dorens completely gentrified than a new crop of uncouth men appeared.

Vincent Van Doren's wealth grew out of young America, which was expanding explosively. He was part of the mercantilist period, where trade boats, ships, and later railroads brought fantastic riches. In the generation that followed his, industrialization took societies to still new levels of prosperity. A large number of men became very rich. And these men were even more aggressive than their predecessors. They persistently bought land on Beacon Hill, building mansions that completely overshadowed each and every existing home. This became so offensive that at one point, the Clarkson Ballroom's popularity faded. Across America, unimaginable wealth was accumulating in the treasuries of men like John D. Rockefeller, Andrew Holden, J. P. Morgan, Jay Gould, and countless others like them who fueled the industrial revolution. It was not unlike the 1990s, when similar wealth was created among legendary traders on Wall Street, and among inventors of new ways to use computers, as well as successful investors in the trillion-dollar healthcare industry, not to mention crooks who stole money in previously unrecorded quantities, hundreds of millions, sometimes billions of dollars, some caught, most not.

Boston's blue-blood society viewed the new prominence of industrialists as akin to the invasion of the barbarians. In Europe, with their newly created barrels of dollars, they were grabbing everything that wasn't tied down. Paintings, sculpture, jewelry, furniture, tapestries, silverware, possessions that had belonged to aristocratic European families for generations were hauled off to America. Castles belonging to lords, barons, and counts were sometimes stripped down to bare stone. It wasn't just their belongings. In England, Ireland, Scandinavia, Italy, they lost the subjects of their manors, whole boroughs of people, people whom their families had counted on for hundreds of years, people whose families they once counted as their own, those who had farmed their land, generation after generation, those who had been connected to their land. It was where their subjects were born and where they were buried. It was where they belonged. Their parents and grandparents had worked this land, and their grandparents' parents and grandparents. Yet given the choice, more confident of survival, they left this land as if it meant nothing to them. They left forever. Not just them but also the townspeople, including masons, smiths, and craftsmen of all varieties, went to work in better paying mines or factories in the cities. Or they went to America. The land-rich but penniless aristocrats had no choice but to sell and sell.

With this kind of power, not surprisingly the new industrial barons were convinced that the future belonged to them. And the past was also theirs, all of it, at least what was left of it in the form of the things that they now owned. Only they didn't just want things. They wanted what went with it, a history longer lasting than the span of their lives. Their future required a solid foundation, a better history, the past rewritten. This is confusing to people who haven't been in their position. It is natural to be shocked, to ask why someone would want anything more than they have, if they already have more than anyone else. It has something to do with permanence.

Down the coast from Boston, in New Haven, much of Yale's campus was built in the 1920s and 1930s, some in the 1950s, with neo-Gothic architecture modeled after that of the great English universities. You might swear the buildings were a thousand years old. Some of the windows were intentionally cracked to give the appearance of authenticity. It is very beautiful, but, more important, the illusion of its age creates a treasured aura of substance.

Thanks to Belize, the Clarkson Ballroom developed that aura. It makes the shiny, lavish modern makeovers of other grand hotel rooms in America seem tawdry. Today its caretakers snobbishly cluck their tongues as they tell you that the Clarkson was never a convention center, nor, they claim, will they ever let it become one. They point out that the people who came to the Clarkson defined American royalty. Boston Society was the crème de la crème. They could trace their lineage to the *Mayflower*. Pilgrims by choice, principle rather than destitution brought them here. That changed. The acid test of status became whether what you had was what everyone else wanted, not pedigree. Later, other men of lofty status, American sports heroes, also ate the breakfast of champions. Robber barons, as they came to be labeled by muckraking journalists, ate the breakfast of champions and dinner, too.

No one in Boston knew much about Vincent Van Doren's private life, but everyone sensed something was amiss. At first, his visits were events, a reason for De Vries and his employees to spiff up. But as the visits became numerous and commonplace, even the employees became suspicious. "Why?" the whisperers asked. "Why Boston?" The leading theory was that it was close enough to New York to be accessible and far enough from his wife so that she could not easily drop in on him. Van Doren strayed many times—all over the world. Particularly when he was young, his body's needs overpowered his restraint. Like a sailor, he was rumored to have the proverbial woman in every port. But Boston was different. It was assumed the explanation for his love affair with his hotel in Boston had to have been Belize. The question was how far they had gone.

One version of the gossip was that he never declared his love, although others emphasize that if that is possible, she must have noticed the way he looked at her. However, everyone looked at Belize that way, so she may not have been aware of it. Some tell of a quick, furtive embrace, which frightened both of them, ending it right off. Nonsense to all of this, the current manager of the Van Doren Hotel insists. Others on his staff agree. Rumors are a waste of time. They acknowledge they may be good for business. They bring the curious, especially those who come to the hotel to step inside the Clarksoon. Current management, however, has little doubt that the hotel was a business venture through and through, requiring every bit of the time Van Doren chose to give to it. But then again, why should this kind of practical analysis by management have a better grip on the facts? Businessmen always claim they are the only realists. Yet busy men miss all kinds of things that are obvious to others.

Chapter 4

In May of 1858, Vincent is accompanying Belize to Paris to shop for the hotel. They are on his recently built ship, the *Julia,* between New York and Marseille. Vincent has been busy with meetings and inspections, checking that everything is running as it should. The presence of Belize is having an added effect on him. He feels younger. He can't help it. An earlier trip on his yacht to Europe with his family, while tense and unsatisfying, had set his mind to go on this venture. England's preoccupation with the Crimean War offered him a time frame to go into competition with the Cunard Line, so he took it. The three ships he launched have been losing money, which makes him uneasy. For now, however, with Belize on board, his pride in being the owner of the *Julia* is overriding his usual concerns about profitability.

As Van Doren enters the boiler rooms, his chest throbs with the power of the engines– his engines! The advanced power plant is superior to those of any other ships on the seas. Despite his lack of formal education, Van Doren designed it. Belize's presence has made him attentive to other details, the shining brass, the polished wood, everything immaculate. The *Julia* has the finest captain on the Atlantic, perhaps in the world, R. B. Smith. Though he would never admit it,

Captain Smith's calm, commanding English demeanor is giving Van Doren unexpected pleasure. So are the carefully chosen sailors, who are noticeably energetic and disciplined. The last few days, he has more than once wondered what his mother would think if she were traveling on this ship, the largest on the Atlantic Ocean. How would his father, the old geezer, have reacted to the fact that his ship holds the record for crossing the Atlantic, nine days, one hour? He wishes they were alive. There are times he sees his life as a fulfillment of his little-boy dreams. He speaks of it to no one, though Julia would understand if he spoke to her about it. Their shared dreams during the early years ended when the necessities of supporting their seven children required he tone down his personal pleasures. By now, his children are adversaries as often as they are partners. He prefers being gruff with Julia. She would see sentimental feelings as weakness, a victory for her.

They are seated at the captain's table. Seated to the right of Belize is Mrs. Mary James, originally from Albany, New York. Belize and Mrs. James are very busy in conversation, mainly about Paris sites that her children might enjoy. Van Doren is seated across from Mrs. James. Her husband had to remain in their stateroom with a touch of seasickness.

An aide moves behind Captain Smith and whispers in his ear. The captain pats his lips with his napkin and rises, addressing his comments to Van Doren.

"My apologies for the interruption. A small matter has come up that needs my attention."

"Would you like me to go with you?" Van Doren asks.

"Absolutely not. It is a misunderstanding that I have to straighten out. Please enjoy your dinner."

They sit silently as he leaves.

Mrs. James is the first to speak. "What could have happened?"

"I am sure it is nothing to be concerned about," Van Doren says loudly enough for the entire table to hear.

Soon private conversations have resumed.

Belize addresses Van Doren. "Vince. Mrs. James is from Albany. Didn't you used to go there often?"

He nods "Yes, I used to have business in Albany, quite a lot. It's a fine city."

"My family and my husband's family are from Albany," Mrs James tell him. "But actually our address is now Twenty-one Washington Place, in New York."

"Really? I live at Twelve Washington Place."

"Yes, I know. People talked when you built your town house."

"Talked about what?"

"Oh, nothing. Chitchat. I suppose that is the price of being well known."

Vincent face does not reveal satisfaction with her compliment. He harrumphs a bit, then quickly follows with a question.

"The James family from Albany. I believe your husband's father, William, did business with me thirty, thirty-five years ago, or one of his associates. Wasn't he involved with the Erie Canal?"

"Perhaps. I'm not sure."

Belize smiles broadly. "Neither of you know each other and you live across the street from each other. New York is a strange place."

"Yes, it is," Vincent replies. "Still, it's funny we've never run into each other on Washington Place. I suppose that is the price of living there. No one goes for a stroll. Out the door and into the carriage."

"It could be us. We are not home that often. My husband, Henry isn't happy unless he is traveling somewhere."

"He travels for business?"

"No. He despises business. His father did enough of that to last five generations. So did my father. My husband lectures."

"On what?"

"Mostly spiritual topics."

"He's a preacher?"

"Yes. Only he doesn't believe in any specific religion. He quit Princeton Theological Seminary because the more he studied, the further he felt from God. You have heard of the Transcendentalists, Ralph Waldo Emerson, Thomas Carlyle? They feel God is in every person, in every tree."

"Is he in the dirt?" Van Doren says gruffly.

She smiles. "I suppose. You will have to ask my husband. Actually, he will be lecturing in Paris. You must come to a lecture on Transcendentalism."

"Transcenden . . . I'm not good with five-syllable words."

"The Transcendentalists—you've never heard of them?"

"Sorry, no, I don't have much time for reading or lectures."

Belize adds cheerfully, "Your husband sounds like he does a lot of deep thinking."

"Oh, he does. The answers he is seeking are like food and air to him."

"That must be interesting," Belize says reassuringly.

"Very! You should hear him talk about peace and love between brothers. He can be very compelling. He thinks competition brings wars. It gets in the way of people understanding one another. That is what he has against business."

Vincent cuts in. "I'm not sure about that. In business, competition is the name of the game. It's what makes it work, everyone trying to outdo every one else. It brings out the best. It doesn't bring love but it brings respect. Businessmen understand one another very well. They wouldn't have it any other way."

"It can get nasty, though, can't it?"

"Well, men are men, but that's fair enough," Van Doren replies. "You just have to accept from the beginning that beating the other guy means he could have beaten you."

"Exactly. That is what my husband wants to avoid. He disliked that quality in his father."

"They didn't get along well?"

"Like oil and water. Two very different men. Both outstanding in their own way. But opposite. My husband wants to avoid that with our children. He's made himself totally available to them."

"But doesn't his work take him away?"

"That is why our whole family is on your ship. We are off to Europe again. So far, we have lived in Switzerland and England, and this time it will be France."

"Lucky children—no school."

"Yes, but they are very well educated. We have a tutor, and my husband is their teacher. Besides, he feels you can learn as much riding on a tram as in a classroom. Especially a tram in Paris."

"Must be nice to be able to teach your children yourself. It takes a lot of time. I have seven of them. I wish I had the time."

"Fortunately, my husband's father left him the means to live life as he pleases."

"Sounds like Mr. James's father was a kind man," Belize says.

Noticing that two of her boys have entered the dining room, Mrs. James calls out to them. "Henry, William." She waves her hand at them. They have not spotted her yet.

"Fine boys. How old?" Van Doren asks.

"Henry is fifteen and William is sixteen."

"So they just travel with you?"

"Yes, our home is wherever we are traveling."

"A man after my own heart."

She waves for the boys to come forward, but they stay back and motion for her to join them.

"Well, I'm afraid my husband is not doing too well. I'll have to attend to him."

She holds out her hand to Van Doren. "Mr. Van Doren?"

"My pleasure."

"I'll mention to my husband that I met you. He is very impressed by this ship. When he read of your record breaking, he insisted on booking on the *Julia*."

"I'll be happy to give him a tour. He can bring the boys."

As soon as Mrs. James is gone, Vincent cannot contain himself.

"Henry James. He's quite a character. I'm sure his father, William, is rolling over in his grave. He was an immigrant and through hard work made a lot of money. Apparently, he specified in his will that his inheritance depended on his son settling down. Henry, Mr. Peace and Love, got a good lawyer and put an end to that. He was able to break the will and has been living off his father's money ever since."

"Interesting."

"Very. I would call that noncompetitive, grabbing your father's money after he is gone, then looking down your nose at businessmen."

Chapter 5

The next morning, Belize is on the ship's deck with a book, bundled up in a blanket not far from the bridge. It is noon, late in May. The sun is brilliant and warm, but the sea air is still nippy. She can see Vincent guiding the captain's wheel, the captain nearby with a half smile, both sharing the pleasure they are getting from the sextant, which is state-of-the-art. Van Doren calls out his readings to the captain, who enters them into the navigational log. She looks out at the ocean, endlessly in every direction its stunning brightly lit deep navy color surrounds them. She wonders how many years it took before Van Doren did not feel lost at sea. For centuries ships have been able to travel thousands of miles without landmarks yet are able to know exactly where they are. Van Doren has left the bridge and is coming toward her.

Belize is planning her campaign. Before they decided to go to Paris, Van Doren had been so impressed with what she had done in the hotel that he told her he was giving her free rein.

"Make the hotel your hotel. Make it a French hotel. Make it as nice as any hotel in Paris."

That is what he said. She isn't completely sure what he meant. Of course, she would like to make the hotel on the level of Le Grande, perhaps far nicer, but in his businesses he has a reputation for liking to make money, not spend it. The first test of his offer will be two very large Persian rugs to be placed at the entrance to the Clarkson Ballroom. She has caught his attention. Shading her eyes, she gestures with her other hand for him to join her. Van Doren walks toward her. With her eyes, she signals for him to take the deck chair next to her, which he does.

Vincent shudders a bit, blows into his hands, shaking off the cold.

"Are you all right?" she asks.

"Yes," he says emphatically. He takes a deep breath. "I love ocean air. Especially when I've been on land for too long." He takes another breath, feeling the cool air moving into his lungs.

"It's something, isn't it?"

"It is."

"I am actually a simple man. Just breathing like this gives me more satisfaction than doing almost anything else."

"More than the moon over the ocean?" she asks.

"That's nice, too."

"More than the sunset last night?"

"You're enjoying the voyage?"

"Very much. I never traveled first-class before. And this boat. Everyone is talking about it."

He continues to blow into his hands.

"You look cold. You should get a blanket."

"I have my flask of brandy. What are you reading?" he asks.

"A book on the rugs of Isfahan."

"Isfahan? Where is Isfahan?"

"In Persia. I told you about the two rugs I want to get for the entryway to the Clarkson. I want them to be very special."

"Yes. It's a good idea. Rugs would look nice there. You should do it."

"I want to get the best."

"I don't think that will be a problem. Everyone is talking about what you've done so far. If you think those rugs should be the best, we will get the best."

"Thank you."

"So, what is it about rugs and Isfahan?"

"In the sixteenth century, the very finest rugs were made in Isfahan. According to this book, they have never been surpassed."

"You can get them in Paris?"

"Of course. The most beautiful rugs are in Paris."

"Why Paris?"

"Because Paris is Paris. We crave beauty. We worship artists."

"But rugs?"

"Yes, rugs."

"I've been meaning to ask you. Why is it that Parisians are so interested in luxury? You know, throughout England factories are springing up that make decent things cheaply, lots and lots of things. What they manufacture becomes affordable for the average person. The French are much less interested in that. Your countrymen feel it is more important to sell luxurious things."

"I don't know why. You think the French are wrong?"

"Wrong or right, it is just the way things are. . . . So the nicest rugs can be found in Paris?"

"Certainly, the most beautiful. Did you know that Persia's greatest artists worked on rugs?"

"For instance, who?"

"They don't have names. Some of the rugs we will be looking at are three hundred years old."

"Really."

"Their names are forgotten. They never expected them to be remembered. I like that."

"So, do I," he replies. Discussions about art and artists ordinarily irritate Vincent, especially when he is with people who get snooty about their taste. But Belize's passion for artistic things has the opposite effect. Perhaps it is because it isn't art that interests her so much as beauty. Her roses, her lip rouge, her shoes, they are all part of that. She has told him she doesn't like many English painters, or Spanish painters, because they are less interested in pretty people. The French, on the other hand . . .

"So what have you learned from your book?"

"You want the short version or the long version?"

"The long. If I am going to learn something, I might as well really learn about it."

"Really?"

"Especially here. All this time on our hands. I have complete faith in the captain."

"And this ship. This beautiful ship."

"So the long version it is."

She begins to tell him what she's read. "Persian rug making began thousands of years ago among nomads in the desert. They provided warmth at night, a luxurious floor, and a bed in the middle of nowhere. It wasn't long before the women who made them began to make them decorative. Eventually, rug making became a central part of the women's lives. You know women's need to talk to one another. When their other work was done, mothers and daughters and grandmothers would sit together and weave for hours at a time. They'd gossip, share memories, fill each other in."

Belize looks up at Vincent self-consciously, like she has been talking silly talk, trivializing what women are about.

"Go on."

"You're sure?"

"Yes. It's interesting."

"Each family had their secret recipes for dyes. They'd boil huge pots of flowers and roots. Some family's rugs are known for their extraordinary shades of red, others for blues or yellows, and some family's colors went perfectly together. The really good dyes fade very little over years and years. We now know there are dyes that lasted centuries. Sometimes, when a family line died out, no one could figure out how certain artisans were able to achieve the colors that they did. Their secrets died with them."

"Really?"

"There is something about parents working with their children. You want to teach them the right way to do something. And they want to show you they can. And then some. But the main thing is to make sure your discoveries, what you have learned about making your rugs remains, just as you have continued what your parents taught you. Over the generations, the rugs became nicer and nicer. As expected, in my family, there were recipes for certain dishes, and every generation added improvements, but you know about the French and food."

"Yes, you are very serious about your pleasures."

"As the Persians are about making rugs."

His eyes become fastened on a color plate in the book. She hands the book to him. He looks at it more closely, then hands the book back.

"It takes years to make a large rug like that, doesn't it?"

"The rugs we are going to look at took close to twenty years to weave."

"You've folded down the corner of that page. What is on that page?"

"You want me to read it?"

"Yes."

"'Since the tribesman were illiterate, eventually the rugs began to be a form of writing. They turned to them as a way to tell their stories in pictures. Some of the rug weavers depicted scenes with powerful emotions attached to them, their fortunes and troubles, their parents in heaven, a passionate moment of love. Sometimes they were inspired by a vision.'"

As she reads, he rests his eyes on her in a way that isn't possible in ordinary conversation. She has the grace of someone who performs on the stage.

She looks up at him. "Did you ever feel the need to do that, portray something that has affected you?"

"Absolutely, certain stories I tell over and over again. It bothers my children, but each time I repeat them, I savor them more and more."

His voice is gentle. Van Doren doesn't usually talk like this. Belize is very aware of it.

She says, "It must be nice to make something that emerges from your spirit, which comes to life when other people share it. It's like a part of you comes back to life."

"It's funny. Lately, I've been thinking about that kind of thing."

"You have?" she asks.

"I think about leaving something behind that is permanent, that will continue after I am gone."

"Like what?"

"I'm not sure. But I think about it."

"Well, we have our children."

"Perhaps, but . . . I don't know. Sometimes I get the feeling my children mainly are thinking about what they are going to get from me when I am gone. That is the downside of having a lot of money. No. I am thinking about something else."

"Like what?"

"I'm not sure, but especially lately. My father died at fifty-nine. That is when all these thoughts started, a year ago, when I reached fifty-nine. But continue reading. You were saying some of the rugs makers were great artists."

"Some of the rugs are extraordinarily beautiful."

"Especially the ones in Paris," he teases.

She smiles at him as she continues. "'In the towns and cities, the rugs eventually became like jewelry, a place to keep the family's wealth. The court of Cyrus the Great, who founded the Persian monarchy over twenty-four hundred years ago, was said to be bedecked by magnificent carpets.'"

"Twenty-four hundred years ago?"

"Yes. And imagine, for twenty-four hundred years, they have been getting better and better at making rugs. A hundred generations."

She reads on. "'As early as the sixth century, the rugs were being exported.'"

He loves her wonderful full French lips as they shape her words. Her tongue occasionally wets her upper lip.

"'Neighboring countries but also people from far away knew about Persia's rugs and wanted them. Even when the Mongols invaded—they destroyed everything they could.'" She purses her lips before hurrying to the next sentence. He can't take his eyes off of them. "'They randomly slaughtered people. With great satisfaction, they grabbed the heads they had cut off by the hair and threw them into piles, which they then admired. But the rugs were handled carefully as treasures.'"

She takes a deep breath. Then she murmurs, "I don't think I want to go to Persia."

"I don't think that happens anymore." Van Doren reassures her.

"You're sure?"

"Well, I hear they still like to cut off heads. But you French perfected it with the guillotine." He smiles. In that moment, she senses his cynicism, but it does not put her off.

"That was my grandparents' generation."

"Did they tell you about the Revolution?"

"They stayed on the farm. Like me, they were uninterested in politics."

His voice is warm again as he asks her to read on.

"'Among his few graces, the conqueror Tamerlane spared rug artisans from his warriors' swords. He had them sent to his palaces in Turkistan. He had big plans for the rugs. Following his reign, every generation of shahs understood that the rugs could bring fortunes to the kingdom.'"

As she reads, the light catches Belize's eyes, momentarily making them glisten as they move back and forth. She looks up at him.

Those eyes! He feels himself being pulled toward them. He could leap into them. They are the color of the ocean, blue, blue blue. He could drown in them.

"Sure this isn't boring you?"

"Not at all. Continue."

Her tone has moved up a notch. "'The climax came with the Safavid dynasty in the sixteenth century. When Shah Ismail occupied the throne in 1501, he began laying the foundation for what was to become a national industry that was the envy of surrounding countries. . . .'"

She looks up again.

"Read more?" she asks.

"Yes. Stop asking."

"Okay, as you wish." She continues: "'The most famous of the kings of this era, Shah Abbas, more than any one, transformed the industry, bringing it from the tents of the wandering nomads into the towns and cities. In Isfahan—'"

"Ah, Isfahan."

"Yes and Paris has the finest collection of rugs from Isfahan."

"That's what your book says?"

"No, but it does." She smiles knowingly. "'In Isfahan, which Shah Abbas made his capital, a royal carpet factory was established. He brought the finest artists to prepare designs to be made by the best craftsmen. By then, men had begun to make rugs. He paid them extremely well. They were as important to him as his generals.'"

He tries not to reveal where he is, but his eyes linger over her long, graceful fingers, her finely manicured nails. Then her thick black hair holds his attention. If she notices she might consider him an old fool. Fortunately, he can plainly see she is enjoying the way he is looking at her.

"'During Shah Abbas's lifetime, the art of carpet weaving achieved its pinnacle.'" She looks up at him again. She speaks to his state. "I promise you. We will find in Paris the nicest rugs from Isfahan."

"Does it mention any particular rugs?"

She turns back a few pages, puts her finger on a line.

"'The best-known carpets of the period, dated 1539, come from the mosque of Ardabil and, in the opinion of many experts, represent the summit of achievement in carpet design.'"

Half seriously, he asks, "Can those rugs be brought to Paris?"

"I doubt it. "

He speaks not very differently than he spoke as a little boy "Don't be too sure. If you're willing to pay enough, you can buy almost anything."

"That would be nice. Very nice." She answers sensing that she has his full attention, Her excitement on her inside is producing what it always does, her smooth as silk persona.

When they finally get to Paris, many of the sixteenth-century Isfahans are, as the book described, like paintings. The two of them are in a store, with rug upon rug piled high.

"Take a look at this, Vincent. These two go together. They are the right size. Feel it."

He does as he's told. Pure tufted silk. Thick but tight. It feels so soft!"

She is mentoring him and he likes it.

"The motif is light and airy. Not what you might expect from a rug."

The rug depicts a young woman dressed in a bright garnet top, leaning backward at an alluring angle while sitting against a tree. She is wearing a green waistband and a yellow skirt. A pink-and-black kerchief is tied around the back of her jet black hair. The exposed tree branches form an intricate network that fills the background. At her feet is a man making offerings. Her face is vaguely depicted compared to her clothes and the background.

Belize speaks softly. "The man who created this loved beautiful things, perhaps more than people. What do you think of the color?"

"It is a damned nice rug," he says in a wise-guy way. Belize is unperturbed. She can see that he is taken with it.

"Ask them how much."

She translates the merchant's answer. "Sixty thousand francs."

He stares at the merchant and laughs. "You can build fifteen houses for that money. Tell him that."

She translates this and the merchant's reply. "He says the price is for the two rugs. There is nothing like these two rugs anywhere in the world. Rugs of this quality come along once in a lifetime." Her eyes plead with Van Doren.

"Tell him fifty-three thousand francs."

She is thrilled by the merchant's answer. Van Doren is thrilled by the look that she gives him when she realizes the rugs will be in the hotel.

Today those rugs, at the entry to the Clarkson Ballroom in Boston, are almost as famous as the "Ardabil" carpet, now in the collection of the Victoria and Albert Museum. One hundred and fifty years later, students still visit the Clarkson to see them. The same can be said for the tapestries, which Belize got a first glimpse at on the second day of their shopping. Many years later, the Metropolitan Museum of Art inquired about the tapestries after they borrowed them for a show. The curators had never seen anything of comparable quality.

"What do woman want?" Freud asked, half in frustration, half in good humor. Are gifts the gateway to a woman's heart? If they are, Van Doren has the potential to be the greatest gift giver of them all. And indeed, the purchase of those rugs had a dramatic effect on Belize. It was the way he said yes as much as the fact itself—no misgivings, not a trace of hesitation. He seemed as excited as she was. She had suspected, she had hoped, she had daydreamed about the possibility of this moment actually happening being able to buy things for the hotel at this level of quality. It still has come as a surprise

When her aunt visited her, on her first night in Paris, Belize told her to tell her mother that she was happy. It was the first time she had ever used that word with her mother. Six months later, she wrote to her mother herself to say that she was happy. She always thought of it as a silly description, meant for people satisfied by a glimpse of a passing emotion, but wishing to extend it in their minds. But the truth is, Belize was exactly that, happy, starting with this trip, and it continued for years and years. There were so many things to buy.

Van Doren also was affected by the purchase of the rugs. He had been attracted to other women, but it never lasted beyond sexual gratification. This was something else. Maybe it was going into the ocean steamship business. Maybe he sensed that he was running out of time. Or maybe it was simply the look she gave him when he gave his approval for the rugs. The look on her face stayed with him so powerfully that he craved to have it repeated.

There is no mystery about his desire. Any man would delight in having the ability to satisfy a woman as beautiful and passionate as Belize. Bringing her to fulfillment would have satisfied anyone capable of bringing her there. Men's insecurity about their manhood places bringing the woman they love to sexual fulfillment on a special, intimate plane. Buying something of this magnitude for Belize, thrilling her, was not different in kind. At that moment, she felt complete, happily possessed. And Vincent was the man who brought her there.

Throughout the trip, they went to shops and galleries, to artists' homes, to importers, to merchants of every variety, wherever the trail traveled by exquisite merchandise led them. The extraordinary sums that Van Doren was spending rearranged his psychology. Normally, the only comparable satisfaction was adding up his net worth in his mind, a number that kept growing and growing and sent him off to many fine nights of restful sleep. He wasn't used to afternoon delights. He wasn't used to the satisfaction of spending his money in a way that made him feel richer. Van Doren is used to being in control of almost every situation. That ceased to exist when he was with her. Again, and again, the experience was the same. He was thrilled when he thrilled her. He had never before gone there with another person. His will, his intelligence completely disappeared.

He swam in a sea of her desires and frustrations. He hoped to see through her eyes, and increasingly it happened. He listened to her thoughts about the rugs. Too blue, not a deep-enough gray, brown undertones. She wants it. He wants it for her. Then she doesn't, disappointing him because he had rapidly grown to like it, had even pictured where he thought of placing it in the hotel, something she usually did.

He was in her orbit. Her *hows* and *whys* and *maybes* became his. Every consideration and reconsideration about purchases for the hotel, pulled him to her. He was having a great time shopping. It had been years and years; he couldn't remember when he had last had a good time, let alone a great time, doing anything. Perhaps never. For Dutch businessmen, great times are not their idea of a life well spent. Or an afternoon. Or the day after that.

One day led to the next. They bought paintings, furniture, fixtures. Her wonderful choices weren't just due to the fact that she had the money to buy anything in the world that could be bought. Yes, shopping with the money of one of the richest men in the world was not a common experience, which made it especially wonderful. But, it wasn't only that. As with her flowers, her passion played the key role in her decisions. She'd enter a shop and suddenly it was there. No one could have predicted, including her, how strong this passion could become. It was not usually apparent. As always she seemed self- possessed, self-denying, hard at work. "Eats like a bird" would be the verdict of those who observed her cravings. True enough. But there was no other way to explain her rapture. She had been starving for this.

Three o'clock on a Thursday afternoon, they sit on a very private park bench surrounded by rows of tulips. Both of them are exhausted, having gone through dozens of items that day. This very bench had been one of Belize's favorite spots when she had lived in Paris. The garden beds constantly changed with new flowers. Not least among this spot's charms was that few people came here. It was almost impossible to find. It had been twenty years since she had last been here, but when she brought Vincent there, she could have found it the in the dark. Which is not surprising. There was no lamppost. It was usually dark when she came here. Which is how it became her spot. Night after night she remained here long after the sun went down.

She discovered the bench serendipitously, a month or two after she had first come to Paris. She had gotten lost one evening and happened upon it. She sat and spent hours in a melancholic swoon. Somehow that was comforting. Subsequently, she came here many times, repeating the experience.

Fourteen is an age when loneliness can be made poignant by beauty. It can become almost enjoyable, like listening to the blues—misunderstood yet again, but oh how the soul sings. Surrounded by the garden's flowers, she was comforted, even as her longing was intensified. The bench was her nunnery, her safe place, a place to yield, for the moment, to where her imagination liked to wander. It was a necessary antidote for where she too often lived.

She can too easily be violated. It was not her fault and it wasn't the fault of the men whose lives crossed hers during those years, simply a consequence of the fact that women like Belize, dazzlingly ripe with youth, must invariably learn to factor protection into the equation of their lives. Perhaps it was being without family, without school. Perhaps it was the tension of her difficulties with her father. But refuge was essential, and she found it here. And so, her desire to belong to a man, and her fear of them, infused the surrounding gardens with her passions. That is how it began. Flowers were safer than men, although as fickle in bringing satisfaction.

She had been a long time away. Vincent had been through this park many times before on his trips to Paris, but he was always in a hurry, always had a purpose, if nothing else to get exercise or take in the fresh air. He had long ago forgotten how to linger.

A cardinal chirps away as it rests on the limb of a dogwood hanging over the bench. She points it out to Vincent. By example she shows him how to listen to the dialogue the cardinal is having with its mate. It is a rare moment, letting down his guard and indulging his own melancholy. He has a fine walking stick bought for him by Julia, but he hasn't really noticed it until, sitting here, he studies its carving. The young Julia passes through his mind.

Belize speaks gently. "After you catch your breath, there is a café I want to take you to at the corner of the park. Would you like a little coffee and pastries to revive you? I'm sure you have not tried all of our pastries."

He says nothing. He ordinarily eats sparingly, but Belize can see hints that he is interested. She quietly unwraps a small statue they had bought and holds it up, studying first one side, then the other, trying out different angles, hopeful that her initial satisfaction will be repeated. It is. Perhaps it is the expression on her face at that moment, or perhaps it is inevitable, but his capitulation has become so complete that he is unaware of being captured. A place in his heart has opened, his fear and caution swept aside by the cadences of her voice, stroking, stroking—he doesn't allow himself to think about it as love. Not in a serious way. That would be disastrous. This was his nephew's wife, his favorite nephew. But the flowers were affecting him, too.

How could they not? He is no different from anyone else in her presence. Her soul electrifies not only her own vision but that of anyone with her. An old part of him is coming back to life, the intensity of the earliest, most thrilling, days of his youth, hidden from view, lying with Julia in the forest near their homes, discovering each other's bodies for the first time. He tightens. He will not allow it.

Belize holds the statuette in front of Van Doren, positioning it at an angle for him that matches the angle she finds most perfect.

"What do you think?"

He says nothing. She brings her hand down and carefully rewraps it. He sits quietly, listening to the birds singing.

"What are you thinking about?"

"Nothing."

"Nothing?"

He hesitates for a moment, then speaks. "You remind me of Julia. She's the only other person who ever got me to walk into shops."

"Is that so terrible? Am I robbing time from more important things?"

"Let's just say that by my usual accounting, this goes in the minus column, not the plus column."

"Oh." Her face drops. She doesn't understand his meaning. He sees that.

"No, actually I like it. I liked it with Julia, too," he quickly adds. "We went to junk shops. We had little money. But it was the same."

"What do you mean?"

"Finding things that will work. Fixing things up. When we bought our first inn, it smelled awful. It was a tavern for river rats. Julia made it nice. I liked helping her."

He sighs, as if Julia were dead. Perhaps she is dead, at least *that* Julia, the one he had been so in love with when they worked together on the inn.

"What happened between you?"

"I don't know." He truly doesn't know. He had his business, and that had always come first in his plans, but also in her plans. Not pleasure. Julia, even more than Vincent, did not understand pleasure as a goal. Business before pleasure was implicit in everything they did. Because both of their families had known very hard times, the original purpose of Van Doren's striving was to get a margin of safety for them. He originally assumed the long hours, the financial gambles were for them. But eventually he could no longer fool himself. His fantasy of the family's connectedness and what his actual family turned out to want were two different things. He realized his children weren't consulted on what he sought to give them and so, perhaps, he was bound to fail. He experienced their reaction as ingratitude, when, in fact, the problem was his original assumption of generosity. But in that, he was like a lot of other fathers, disappointed that what he worked for meant so little to them. The bickering, the tension when they were all together could be unbearable. He had a yacht built, for a voyage to Europe, a fantastic yacht. It, too, had been a disappointment to him. It was his final try. Nothing seemed right.

His married relationship with Julia had started so well. When they were fixing up their inn, when Julia lugged back junk for him to polish or repair, her vision and his united them. His elbow grease and hers, his scrubbing and hers, when they had gotten rid of the beer smells, cleansed the floor of the last remnants of urine, opened the windows, brought in fresh air, it was almost as if they erased their families' history, generation after generation of want.

The Van Dorens had a few very nice things, things that Belize might have liked. Both his family and Julia's had always been proud of a Delft vase that had been brought by their ancestors from Holland and carefully preserved in the family for a century. It was finally given to them by the grandmother they had in common. Also the tulips, which every spring were displayed in the vase. The bulbs had multiplied over the course of 150 years. Both their families knew the secret of propagating tulips. Both he and Julia loved tulips. From other conversations, Belize felt she knew Julia well.

"Your wife and I have much in common."

But it wasn't Julia she understood. Julia's presence was once-removed, a shadow, barely alive, dying inside of Vincent. She could only know, only feel whatever Vincent felt about Julia. And that particular Julia aroused sympathy for Vincent. Belize wanted to caress the loneliness she sensed in him, the loss that kept eating away at him. She moved forward innocently. They were old enough and experienced enough to take heed of the warning signs. They could be heading for trouble. But that was out of the question. They both told themselves that their shopping trips would have to do. They were determined to stick to that. And shopping they did and did.

There were similarities between Julia and Belize, but the difference between them was also important. Julia was uncomfortable with the fancy people, felt humiliated when she had to mix with them, embarrassed for herself as well as for Vincent, both essentially the same, crude at their core, having grown up doing farm chores. Julia was satisfied when she could make their inn presentable. Belize's love for beautiful things was her raison d'être. And she rarely doubted that she belonged. Indeed, especially on this trip having Van Doren with her, she felt she had, at last, arrived.

Belize took Van Doren everywhere in France, but especially "her Paris," as she put it, meaning her dream Paris, the places she had previously gaped at from afar. Before leaving for Montreal, she had been a shop girl at Les Trois Quartiers, in the objects d'art section. From the outset, it had been more of a calling than a job. She had been taken to Les Trois when she was twelve, while visiting her aunt Celeste in Paris. It was love at first sight. From that day forward, she knew exactly where she needed to be—as close to her love as she could get.

Belize brought up her Paris trip to her mother repeatedly, sometimes with a dreamy faraway gaze. At first, her mother smiled as she listened, fondly remembering her own teenage foolery, but when it became clear Belize and her father could not exist under the same roof for much longer, Belize's fantasies were turned into a plan. Aunt Celeste arranged for a job working at Les Trois, and everything else followed. It went well. Belize could have been frightened by being sent off to Paris at such a young age, but other than a few butterflies the first hour or two when she arrived in her new home, Belize was excited to get going. Even at sixteen, after she had worked at Les Trois for close to two years, her sense of adventure remained. She was having a passionate affair with most of the items she sold.

In the farmhouse of her childhood, bric-a-brac would have seemed odd. Her father was like Van Doren. Things were things, functional or useless. It was exactly the opposite for Belize. The merchandise in Les Trois Quartiers possessed her. The person in charge of the two large rooms that Belize worked in, Madame Reynaud, was more than happy to be her mentor. Indeed, there could have been no greater gift to the Madame than Belize's enthusiasm. She had started to become bored by her routine. Belize's keen interest reminded her of her own when she began working at Les Trois. Belize revived it. "Chic," "handsome," "amazing," "stunning"— Madame pronounced her judgments to Belize. Belize delighted in them.

They got each other going. While still living at home, after her aunt took Belize to the ballet *La Sylphide,* Belize imagined herself to be Marie Taglioni, a feather of a creature. Years later, her daydream had grown even stronger. At work, when no one was around, Belize would hum the tunes and dance through the room, doing a bow before a stone Buddha, a twirl for the benefit of a marble Apollo (her favorite of the gods). She stroked the smooth brass of one of the lamps. Her fingers registered the lushness of silk. On more than one occasion, unbeknownst to Belize, Madame Reynaud watched sixteen year-old Belize with a full heart.

The store was filled with the very finest products of gifted craftsman from all over the world, from France, Bavaria, Vienna, Brussels, Venice, Geneva, Madrid, Toledo, Florence. Madame Reynaud had her admiring stitching, studying small and large designs. Boldness excited her; meticulous detail was calming. There were certain differences between teacher and student. Belize, for instance, was very fond of Chinese and Japanese crafts. Madame Raynaud was not. To Belize, the absence of froufrou, the simplicity, the tight focus, the lines of steel, the absolute discipline–all hit a chord. Not because this accurately described Belize's habits. If anything, she was precisely the opposite. Discipline would be the last thing that occurred to anyone when confronted by Belize's galloping spirit. But when she did something she loved, she got very good at it. Endless repetition does that when it is something that you love. Maybe it isn't peculiar that she was attracted to a culture so at odds with her personality. Many girls her age want what they don't have, seek to be who they are not. At sixteen, growing up is full of transformations over and beyond being the unfolding of character. Like other girls her age Belize longed not only to change into a person she was not, and might never be, but, more to the point, to possess what she would never own.

The items she loved were so far beyond anything she could afford, they could only be approached through daydream. That didn't present a problem. However unreal fairy tales from her childhood might have been, and usually are for most sixteen-year-olds, they remained unusually alive in Belize, alive with the same delight as a child. Living in her imagination they existed on an exalted plane, far, far better than what Belize, at that age, was being offered by reality.

So whether it was a form of madness, or another manifestation of the infinite ways the mind can dream up to protect the fragile psyche of a sixteen year old, Belize was made up differently than the average person

A modern psychiatrist might have noted her abnormality. The extent to which she retained the fairytale side of her personality made her weirdly off the charts, but on the other hand she could visit enchanted places more often. And on further thought she was not altogether unlike many girls her age on the verge of womanhood, when they first discover the world outside their home. Most girls eventually lose that lavish sense of wonder as they settle into a familiar adulthood, but not Belize. It was more intense from the very beginning and grew from there.

Perhaps it was because she handled things she loved every day. One afternoon, a vase arrived from China that sent her into a hypnotized state. She fought to remain focused as best she could, to remain busy, in this case by dusting the rest of the items in her department. Then dusting them again. But the vase kept calling her back. It had a rich blue glaze with a delicate web of cracks making up the patina. She worshipped the voluptuous curves, perfectly proportioned and molded. Day after day, week after week, her attraction grew. She moved the vase to an inconspicuous location. She kept her back to it constantly. She tried everything to regain mastery over it. Nothing worked.

Nothing until she finally gave in and yielded to it. She first began, at that point, the behavior she was to greatly expand upon in the Van Doren Hotel. She moved the vase throughout the department, anxious to see the effects of its placement. She moved other objects near it, away from it, behind it, until finally an epiphany occurred. Not a spiritual moment in the ordinary sense, but something like the satisfaction that comes to an artist when he is able to possess a beautiful scene that has captured him, change his yearning and hunger for it into his completed rendering.

It wasn't just the vase. The pull of the things she loved was continuous. If she could not buy them, finding the right spot for them would have to do. Her arrangements were the only kind of ownership possible. She would sigh with contentment when she got it right.

The results of her inspirations were no small thing. Eventually, seeing Belize's gift, Madame Raynaud encouraged her to do whatever she wanted in her arrangements. And very soon, one look and customers entering the department knew something unusual was occurring. She had no training, but she intuitively knew what was needed. She searched to find the right combination of color shadings, of shapes that moved and shapes that tranquilly anchored the eye, sizes that stood up and others that drew you down, textures that cuddled the vision, or bounced back at the viewer like polished stone. And always the perfect light. From here, in this department store, through days and weeks of the rituals that she performed for her job, the future Belize was born, the Belize of Boston. Paris had been a practice run. Here she began what she later continued and perfected at the Van Doren Hotel, arrangements of gorgeous things as only the most outstanding Parisian shopkeepers can do. And, by the time she was twenty, word had gotten around among the fashionable. Her section of the store was visited by all the best people. That was the good part.

The bad part was that dress it any way you choose, she was a shop girl. Belize often had the upper hand when mesdames visited her section, simply by being young and beautiful, and possessing her talent. Many of her customers came to depend on her judgment, and gladly told her in subsequent visits about compliments they had received for decisions made by her.

But certain customers made sure she remembered she was a shop girl. It wasn't just at work. From time to time, on her days off, she was occasionally sniffed out by certain shopkeepers at the very best shops who were not fooled by her fashionable outfits and always present personality. They could tell by her shoes. Fine ladies did not wear inexpensive shoes. It was humiliating, and it could be repeated when she least expected it.

Perhaps going hand in hand with their taste, Parisians are especially gifted at looking down at those beneath them. Germans are known for their arrogance when they hold social advantage, the English can extinguish their inferiors by being oblivious of them, but the French are more likely to revel in the details of taste and grace. It took only one or two snubs and she didn't go back for third helpings, which is exactly what the shop owners wanted. Although there were other reasons, it took only three or four incidents for her to first think about moving to Montreal.

One time in particular stood out in her mind. The Chinese vase she loved was completely out of her reach, but she had been determinedly saving for six months, often skipping meals, for a particularly fine mantelpiece clock, at a shop nearby, rumored to have once been in Napoléon's drawing room. Being in the business, she was to receive a discount. She was one month away from owning it. She came, as she always did, to pay it her weekly visit. When she arrived, the Countess of Beaujolais was already there, running her palms along the smooth arches of the clock. The shopkeeper, who, on more than one occasion, had been irritated by Belize's visits, couldn't refrain from the opportunity. Acting superior in the presence of the countess was a temptation she couldn't resist. Until then, she had been polite and businesslike, even friendly to Belize, hoping to make the sale. But instantaneously, that changed. Belize didn't know what hit her. The mocking tone cut right through her.

"Ah, here is our shop girl. . . . Countess, I give to you . . . Your name, mademoiselle?"

"Belize."

"Belize? What kind of name is that?" the shopkeeper asked impatiently.

Belize looked at the ground. She wanted to sink into it.

"It's the name my family used. My formal name is Belle-Elyse."

"Ah. So then why Belize? Why Belize? What does Belize mean?" the shopkeeper repeated to her, as if scolding a child.

"It means nothing."

"So then why not Belle-Elyse?"

"Why not indeed." The countess stepped in. "What is your family name?"

"Moreau."

"Oh. The Moreaus from Auvergne?" asked the countess.

"Yes."

A glimpse from the countess and the shopkeeper raised her eyebrow as if she were cackling. The countess smiled, savoring the delicious morsel of their triumph. Their expressions were not wasted on Belize, who immediately realized there must be no Moreaus in Auvergne. The jig was up. The shopkeeper's voice took on a patronizing, just-before-the-kill howl of victory.

"So, my mystery woman, Belize Moreau, or Belle-Eyse, or whoever you are." Words were not necessary. Their look said it all. You invented yourself. You are not real. Why would you want to do that? What are you ashamed of?

It had reached the point of no return. Literally. Belize hands covered her face as a reflex, as if she had been struck there.

"Pardon," she mumbled as she turned around. She wanted to run, but she left the store with measured steps, hoping to retain a remnant of dignity.

For years, her humiliation burned in her memory, causing her to blush, even though, at the time, it seemed as if she had made a quick recovery. Indeed, with the money she had saved for the clock, she decided that she might as well go after what she truly wanted, the Chinese vase in her department. It would take her a very long time—it was five times the price of the clock. By her calculations, she might have the money for it in eight months to a year. Only there was a formidable problem. What if someone else bought it? Store rules forbade hiding any item for sale. Nevertheless, when she sensed a prospective customer, she did her best to make it look unattractive, putting completely unsuitable flowers in it. Despite her efforts, the vase kept getting serious attention from buyers. There was no way to hide its perfect proportions.

Twice, she had told customers it was already sold. If either of those customers were to have mentioned this to store management, she would have been out of a job. But when she finally had the money, bought the vase, took it home, and made her first flower arrangement, it was all worth it. She at last experienced the consummation of her desire. True, the love it evoked could be measured in hours, or, at most, days. After that, the flowers she had placed in it would wilt. But short love affairs are always the most perfect. The wonderful thing was that her experience could be renewed, gloriously restored again and again, every time Belize brought wonderful flowers to put in it.

On more than one occasion, with good reason, Belize wondered if she had any talent at all. In truth, anyone who put even a single flower in that vase might be similarly impressed by their abilities and turn to flower arrangements with their fascination multiplied. Flowers placed any which way looked so wonderful that this vase might have convinced them that they were blessed with a great gift. Possessing the power to create beauty like that can do it.

Or perhaps these considerations are academic. Whether it was the good fortune of finding this vase or whether it was inherent genius, the very first time she put a flower in that vase, she was swept along a channel that eventually culminated in her masterful creations. And this was years before she learned the secrets of that Japanese master.

She had worked so hard to save the money, existing on day-old bread and meat and vegetables on the verge of spoilage, wearing a coat during the winter that had grown thin. But the vase had been worth every sacrifice. On alternating nights, she would bring flowers home and could be in another world while arranging them. For years, she awakened in the morning and quickly went to the vase to view the flowers she had placed there the previous evening. Often, as she made improvements, she suddenly realized she would be late if she didn't get a move on it. During the day, she would recall her arrangements as others recall a certain look, a moment with their lover. Or she would be bothered. Something was not quite right. On those nights, she would rush home to address the problem, making adjustments until she was satisfied. On her day off, she was a very happy young lady, doing serious arranging, and serious studying of the results. Perfect love. She always got back as much as, or more than she gave. And she gave a lot.

The sacrifices that she had so willingly made for her purchase intensified her excitement with Vincent, when she was able to buy whatever she wanted with one word. She had entered a kind of paradise, with Vincent Van Doren as the maker of her miracles. And let us not ignore the fact that Belize's limitless budget may have saved her soul. What if she hadn't crossed paths with Van Doren? Her inability to own things that she loved had originally inspired her with longing, but eventually youthful desire could have easily eaten away at her and begun to turn into envy. Her desire could have turned back on itself, become bitterness and dissatisfaction, the fate of so many who begin with dreams. She was simply lucky. Van Doren rescued her from a potentially unhappy evolution.

How different it was to return to Paris and be welcomed, to see the very people who had once dismissed her, now servile before the mighty Van Doren. And her! It wasn't just shopkeepers. In later shopping trips, Belize and Vincent were welcome at châteaux for dinner where, in her former life in Paris, she would not have gotten past the outside gate. She loved the preposterous spectacle of the nobility kissing up to this farm boy turned magnate. It was a spectacle. He'd be announced and the counts' and dukes' and earls' hearts skipped a beat. She watched as they waited for a moment to insinuate themselves into a conversation with him, or her, all so that they might get a private meeting with him. She loved the roll of their tongues, their lips as they pronounced the name Van Doren.

Word had gotten out among the nobility. Van Doren possessed extraordinary, unheard-of amounts of currency. Dollars and dollars. Ridiculous amounts. He literally had more money than the entire United States Treasury. Money, in those amounts, made him king. Having guillotined practically all of the counts, viceroys, kings, queens, and princes in France, without true royalty, the result in Paris went as might have been predicted. Given a power vacuum, not brotherhood, liberty, and equality, but a catty, ever-shifting aristocracy of artifice characterized Parisians. If the Eskimos have a hundred words for snow, the French have a thousand phrases to express their taste and superiority. Up in society one day, down in another. In fashion, out of fashion. Paris had already begun the process that had made Parisian obsession with their ever-changing ideas about fine things a defining characteristic, an admired one.

So, in that sense, Belize and Van Doren fit in quite well. Not necessarily, however, because they were nouveau riche. In one respect, they were almost more representative of the old order than the new. Yes, Belize had begun as a typical Parisian and lost badly enough that she had had to leave town. But she had returned as the real thing, meaning Van Doren's money was not going to run out. So, whether she'd made up her name or had been once exposed as a parvenu was irrelevant. She left town in defeat, but made a glorious return. What mattered most was that Van Doren would pay a fortune for an item in any châteaux if he liked it. Ludicrous amounts. Actually, not he. She. If Madame Belize liked something, incredible money could magically appear.

It was all done tastefully. Belize would see something she liked and Van Doren would stop to study it, and very soon the count would offer it as a gift, a memento of their visit. The following morning, Belize would go to pick it up and name a price that was always to the nobleman's liking. The money, of course, was refused. He would insist it was a gift. But there was no way Belize could leave without offering a handsome number of dollars in return. And with great protestations, he would finally relent. With paintings, it was clumsier, but always it was given as a gift, not offered for sale. Everyone knows that the nobility have no great need of bourgeois money.

In private, Belize and Van Doren bluntly referred to their dinners as "shopping for the hotel," but whatever it was, it got the two of them more invitations to gala evenings with their fine-feathered hosts than they could keep up with. Nice friendly notes on embossed cards came all the time, as well as flowers for no particular reason. All said the same thing. Come to my château. Come to dinner. And as if there weren't enough invitations to keep them busy in Paris, eventually nobility came from the neighboring provinces, and eventually invitations came from all over France when they heard that Van Doren was leaving Paris and would sail back from Marseille.

Van Doren had become an honored and esteemed man. As Belize put it, "Money may not buy happiness, but it does buy easy friends." Without a king to set standards, fallen aristocrats from around the world now gathered and tried to hold court. It had also become a city where a rich businessman could buy a family title. True pedigree mattered, the pedigree of having more francs than any other pretender to the throne. While Van Doren was not interested in becoming a nobleman, he enjoyed his royal status every time he appeared with Belize.

It also allowed Belize to visit the château of the Countess of Beaujolais. She found it as memorable as their first meeting. From the start of that evening, the countess stared at

Belize with a vague recollection that she had seen her somewhere before. There was also the name. Belize. A strange name. The count had invited them because he was in a perilous financial situation. His gambling debts had reached a point where he was being hounded by creditors, treated poorly, even by common tradesmen who were becoming tired of his IOUs. The couple had a Delacroix in the main dining room that they knew could fetch enough to pay off all of their debts. Hence the dinner in honor of Monsieur Van Doren.

Belize was uninterested in the painting. She was very interested in the clock below it, above the mantelpiece——yes, the clock rumored to have belonged to Napoléon. When she ran her hand across it, the countess finally placed her. Seeing her interest, Vincent, a short while later, stood before the clock. The count offered to give him the painting.

"I was admiring the clock," said Van Doren.

The countess stepped forward. "I'm sorry, Monsieur Van Doren, but that clock was given to me by my mother," she said.

Belize spoke directly. "That clock, the way it sits right now beneath the painting, they belong to each other."

"Yes. Yes. The two. Let me give you the painting with the clock," said the count. "I would be honored."

"No," the countess said. "I think we should give you this painting and that one next to it as well, both, but not the clock." Belize savored the desperation in the countess's voice. She looked the countess in the eye. The countess could not take it. She flushed.

"Okay, the clock."

"Yes," Belize said smoothly. "How kind of you."

The next morning, the countess herself, rather than her husband's business agent, exacted the best price she could. Normally, Belize didn't bargain. She was absurdly generous. She could afford to be. Whatever outlandish sum she paid it was a drop in a gigantic bucket. But this time, she paid half what the paintings might be worth. One was a Corot landscape, the other the Delacroix. The countess knew what Belize was doing, but at this point, getting the money was more important than her pride.

As time went on, Van Doren showed more interest in the items they were buying. He initially bought things because Belize wanted them. But after a while, Belize would bring him objects to look over and it was impossible not to notice that they were compelling to him as well. And once that took hold of him, his interest deepened. It might even be suggested (with great trepidation) that he was developing good taste. Belize said that to him once, and he didn't contradict her. At home, he despised good taste, hated New Yorkers' and Bostonians' snobbishness about wines, ideas, music, their vapid desire to establish that they were better than others. But with Belize, there was no one to defend himself against. She came from the same social class. So when he was with her, Van Doren could be open to culture, and his refinement proceeded honestly and naturally. And once that door had opened, he began to respond to the layers and layers of emotions that certain of his paintings could evoke in him, especially when he was in her presence. Having her close by did to him what she did to others, sent his senses into an intense receptivity. The world was illuminated around him. Back home, whether he wanted to or not, he invariably played the fool with the swells, but in France, his broken French peppering the charming French lips of Belize made the two of them legendary. Good or bad gossip followed them wherever they went. True or false, small details or larger-than-life tales—no one got tired of examining their debris. Once they left a château on a given evening, all of the other guests might ridicule and imitate them, which only meant that even when they were gone, they still possessed center stage. As far as Belize was concerned, the very best thing about all their invitations was that she got to see some very fine rose gardens, and brought back to Boston the most spectacular specimens.

Van Doren relished being at the hotel when the harvest of treasures from Paris was uncrated, all soon to be at home in their new hotel surroundings. While Belize waited with anticipation and fear, hoping but not sure that an item would be as wonderful as she had remembered it, he was immune. Yes, when she was pleased, she would watch his reaction to see if he was pleased. When she was disappointed, her eyes moved to him for comfort. But either way they were having a good time. It was as if they were playing house, like a wife showing her husband what she had brought home from her day of shopping.

Ernest and Belize had a terrible fight following the first time he caught on to what was happening. After that, her husband stopped going to the uncratings. He accepted Belize's assurances that nothing was going on beyond that, or would go on, but he knew. He knew. Sexual liaison or not, he had become a shadow.

Buying and owning and honoring the objects of Belize's desire went on for decades. Their time together was a fulfillment of her quest. She lived and breathed in every inch of the hotel, in every hallway, in every room. But none more so than in the Clarkson Ballroom, which eventually became the most elegant, the most beautiful location in Boston, the place where the finest people in Boston met.

Belize and Vincent both agreed that the very best thing they owned was the Rembrandt, which hung in the ballroom. In truth, it might not have been a Rembrandt. No one knew who had painted it. But one day, at one of the châteaux, Vincent had stopped in front of this painting and studied it for a long time. The eyes of a man in his sixties, staring out of the canvas, held him there. Belize came to the conclusion, that it was a Rembrandt. She told him that the intimacy of this man's expression could not have been painted by anyone else. Van Doren said he felt as if the man in the painting were alive and about to speak to him. The man in the painting urgently had something to communicate. Only Rembrandt could do that with his paintbrush.

Van Doren didn't mention anything about wanting to buy the painting, but Belize knew. Only years later did he realize what had pulled him to the man in the painting. The way he looked at Van Doren was the way his father sometimes had looked at him after they had reconciled. He had been gone for years. The longer he was dead, the more Van Doren appreciated him. He missed his father. As awful as their early relationship had been, their later connection meant a lot to him. The tense, awful years had almost disappeared. His memories of the two of them during the early years, when Vincent simply belonged to him, when the standards of the outside world meant everything, his embarrassment intruded on his opinion of him. But with Van Doren's triumph over the outside word, others' opinion hardly mattered.

When he was in the presence of this painting, when he looked into the man's eyes, he felt serene. He told Belize about this, and she said, "Good, you said your father wanted to make an impression on the world. We'll put it in the Clarkson Ballroom so he can look out at the fine people that come here and be proud of his son."

Chapter 6

Theories abound, but no one knows for sure how and why the Clarkson came to assume the prominence it currently enjoys. One rumor has it that Vincent Van Doren, at the peak of his power, cherished the Clarkson because of a single episode. In defiance of convention, he is said to have danced openly in the ballroom with the one woman he truly loved. But this is not documented. Moreover, despite this claim, it is impossible to cite the time, the incident, even the woman. Belize's relationship to Van Doren is an unknown. Arthur Howden Lavin, one of Van Doren's biographers, makes no references to Belize.

Nevertheless, the fact is that Vincent Van Doren specified in his will that the keepers of the Clarkson Ballroom must be the hotel's most trusted employees. Belize's daughter Ariana De Vries, head of the hotel from 1902 until 1934, made sure that this stipulation was taken with utter seriousness. Forever was impossible, but she put extraordinary energy into ensuring that Van Doren's will would be persuasive enough to get a good long run. She was a shrewd judge of character. She carefully chose Irene and Ben Wallace as caretakers, to assume responsibility after she was gone. Irene, from day one, was gaga about the beauty of the silverware, the tablecloths, the dishes and wineglasses. And Ben was a good young man with a sentimental disposition. He was like her puppy. At the time they were chosen, they were engaged to be married.

Ariana was confident she had found the right people for the job. But to ensure it, she threw a wedding reception for the Wallaces in the Clarkson Ballroom. For a night, they owned the room. For a lifetime, they would treasure it. They were told their daughters would also be married in the Clarkson. When they came back from their honeymoon, they were given a title that appeared in the hotel directory: Caretakers of the Clarkson. They were well compensated. They had at their disposal any and all workers found necessary to keep the Clarkson up to Ariana's exacting standards. They were devoted, some would say pious. They, in turn, chose their daughter to replace them, and she and her husband were also up to the job.

Today, employees working in other parts of the hotel sometimes joke that the caretakers of the Clarkson are servants in a mausoleum. They say that late at night ghosts inhabit the room. It is jealousy. It is also partially true. Irene and Ben Wallace, caretakers of the Clarkson until 1974, treated the room as if it were a holy relic. They took the T home at night to eat and sleep in a Dorchester apartment. But during the day, they stood grandly with Vincent Van Doren in his room. From an early age, they enlisted their children to help make the Clarkson shine. Van Doren lived through them. And with each generation, this aspect has grown. His spirit doesn't die. He lives in stories, which have multiplied over the years, stories that have been repeated so often that no one can sort out what is true and what is legend. It won't be long until the legends become religion. Indeed, both Irene Wallace and her daughter had the same vision, which awakened them in the middle of the night. Van Doren walked on water. They were certain that meant something.

Monuments usually represent a person's dreams. If the Clarkson embodies Van Doren's dreams, it is worth our attention. For dreams are always revealing and fascinating, particularly because they bear so little resemblance to reality. Dreams are the antidote to reality, filling in for what is missing. They keep us going with hopes of what still might be. In America, they are given an unusual place of honor. Not the past, but our dreams, our hopes for the future, our love of the new have turned out to be our most enduring tradition. When dreams are actually made real, the result can be magnificent, a word often used to describe Van Doren's ballroom. Nevertheless, the Clarkson remains a product of the imagination. Its most assured quality, its elegance, speaks volumes about its history. The room is exactly as it was intended to be. Nothing has changed. Nothing is allowed to be changed. Which is the point worth noting. It protests too much. It conceals, rather than reveals, its true history.

The Clarkson belies the Van Doren family's identity. Let us once again recall that Vincent Van Doren's parents were not from Boston. They lived on a farm. They had dirty fingernails. Manure stuck to the bottoms of their shoes. When they were prosperous, chickens and pets went in and out of their house.

Van Doren's dream, or was the Clarkson Ballroom the product of Belize's will? Or did they both become the same thing?

Mid-May from 1866 well into the 1960s, the Debutante Cotillion Ball at the Clarkson Ballroom in the Van Doren Hotel opened the social calendar in Boston. It was eagerly awaited every year, but particularly in 1875, when the New England winter had punished Bostonians beyond even their endurance. Once again, the crocuses and daffodils had been a tease, making April fools of everyone. For on April 2, Boston was under siege, pounded by its second blizzard in thirty days, this time two and a half feet of snow, drifts of ten feet, temperatures below zero for close to a week.

The blizzard arrived unannounced around midnight. By 3:00 A.M., half the people in Boston were awakened by the howling winds. In the dark, they listened and felt a chill before they tightened the blankets around themselves and drifted back to sleep. The next morning, they were greeted by the chatter of hail striking glass. This brought them to their windows, and actually their first look at the storm contained an element of fascination with the sheer power of nature. However, as the day progressed, the storm seemed to strengthen, and their fascination was replaced by concern. The winds angrily blasted away, moaning and screeching with a vocabulary undecipherable to human intelligence. Giant tree limbs came crashing down, blocking roads, breaking through the roofs of homes and businesses. The second night was worse than the first. When this was repeated still a third night, the storm began to cut away at people's sanity, especially because a number of residents were sure they had felt the earth rumble during the night. There hadn't been a serious earthquake in Boston since November 1755.

Some paced the floor; many more twisted and turned in bed throughout the night, trying not to listen to the wind, not to think, not to do anything other than sleep, the very worst way to fall asleep. By the fourth morning, when the storm still had not let up, some Bostonians had become unnaturally quiet. No one knew what to expect next. In 1875, there was no radio, TV, telephone, or weatherman, no explanation of what, exactly, was happening and when it would end. Fear makes minds work overtime, makes the imagination run wild. Everyone had to make whatever sense they could.

Perhaps the blizzard was punishment for collective sin, for something awful that they had done. The honest among them knew their personal contribution, and this wasn't altogether comforting, but would God be this angry? At what? In a fury, He had once wiped out the world with forty days of rain when the human race had become corrupted beyond forgiveness. Was this the beginning of a forty-day blizzard? Or was it simply an anomaly of nature, an unlucky rolling of the dice, a once-in-a-hundred-years storm? And was that an earthquake last night? If only they could hear what the priest had to say, hear if there was news. Not knowing was the worst of it.

It is fair to wonder why there is so much speculation at such times. But then again, it is to be expected. People think and think when something is wrong. Good thoughts or bad thoughts, valid explanations or nonsense, they think and think until they have found something that makes sense. Whether true or false, it almost doesn't matter. When danger is knocking on the windows, when the wind wildly mocks the ordinary silence of night, what else can people do if they don't speculate? Pace the floor? Climb the walls? Start bickering with each other? Read the *Farmers' Almanac* for the third and fourth time? Collapse heavily into a chair in despair, or spring up like a deer hearing a menacing sound? The people of Boston did all of these things and considered still more theories. None of it was very effective. The truly insane might have done what most would have been tempted to do—attempt to strike back, open the door and scream curses at the storm. The sensible, however, understood that they would be shouting into the void. Their sound would be completely unheard beneath the howling winds.

By the fourth day, those who had earlier learned how to tune out now stared off into space, took a journey inside their minds to familiar places. The less fortunate found crevices from which it might be harder to return. Some people played the piano until they got tired of the same old tunes. Some people prayed; some laughed, or imitated laughter. And when all was said and done, regardless of how they tried to handle it, there was only one true answer to this storm and the winter of 1875: the spring.

To a starving man, a scrap of bread tastes as fine as Belgian chocolate. The same principle applies to the seasons: the worse the winter, the more glorious the spring. A few snowflakes fell in early May, two weeks before the ball, but no one paid it any mind. The snow melted almost immediately. As terrible as things had been during the blizzard and the hard freeze that extended through most of April, the worst had been forgotten after they had sunshine for a week in May, then two weeks, then sixteen glorious days in a row.

Given that the blizzard was still recent, no one was ready to assume they were completely out of the winter, but the evidence was mounting. Profuse dogwood blossoms were a good sign. Then something better, something that often went by unnoticed but this year lit up like fireworks ablaze in the sky. Tulips appeared, followed by azaleas and rhododendron: vibrant colors, gorgeous colors, dazzling reds, purples, crimsons, cranberry, and pinks battled the gray torpor of winter, shook the senses to awaken. From absolute stillness, from a suspended state, from nothingness, life had sprung back into motion. Plants peeked out of the ground, then got down to business. A week or two later, they bloomed. Flowers and more flowers. The brain smiles at flowers even in New England, where smiles are tentative. Especially in New England.

Spring is a parade of flowers in every shape and size, one following another in assigned progression. By the time redbud arrives in the middle of the parade, people's expectations have reached a point where they expect the marvelous. They aren't disappointed. Cherry and crab apple blossoms, peonies, poppies, lupine, roses, a procession varying little from year to year. That year, 1875, because of the long freeze, the emergence of each flower telescoped into a shorter time frame. It had a spectacular effect. Each flower appeared, while the earlier flowers still remained. Belize's flower arrangements were the best they had ever been. Everything appearing all at once, the entire cast together in a finale, leading to a grand crescendo, the Cotillion Ball held in the Clarkson. The ball was the high point, the culminating event. Entering the Clarkson had come to mean that spring was finally irreversible. But it was more. For those caught up in the social calendar, the ball at the Boston Van Doren seemed as if it had been the whole purpose of the parade. Each rite of spring built upon the last prelude, everything leading to this, the grand event. Nature's most beautiful blossoms, dangerously beautiful city blossoms, debutantes, the fairest of the fair, the daughters of pretty women chosen by successful men, all gathered together in the Clarkson Ballroom, where they could be duly celebrated.

They arrived in fine coaches driven by impeccably attired coachmen, with horses that seemed to prance as they appeared from behind the circle surrounding the fountains and came to the grand entryway of the Van Doren Hotel. Those who were simply witnesses to the ball, those without daughters being introduced, entered the lobby with laughter and gaiety. Those who were presenting their daughters tried to seem just as carefree, but that fooled no one. Strain edged their laughter. Each of the young ladies was ushered to a special room with their mothers and servants, where they might prepare for their moment. They were very excited.

If you looked at the faces of the debutantes, you saw children, dreamy, without a clue, which was very desirable.

With the young women dressed in the most beautiful gowns they had ever worn, intimations of the women they might become took hold of their audience. The seeming contradiction of their childish nature and their women's bodies created a powerful tension. Some consider the beauty of virgins the most precious lure. The most desirable quality was not to have a trace of sophistication. Glorious innocence, but with devilish curiosity and flirtatiousness, was perfection.

They were closely studied by every matron in attendance that night. They were a reminder of a place and time where each of those older women had once been. They could remember their own thrill when, at last, they had been invited to the adults' table. As at Christmas time, those who delight in the children's excitement do so because it arouses their own memories. It allows them to recall themselves as children, so they can have Christmas again. In the same way, the debutantes' youth and energy enticed everyone to share it with them, to recall their own younger physical qualities. The debutantes' bodies were still perfect, better than they would ever again be, newly formed, natural, with no thought given to repair. Their noses had not yet grown, nor their lips or ears. Their teeth were shiny white; their hair was thick and healthy where it should be, and peach fuzz everywhere else. The men, young and old, could have looked at them forever, or at least until they were aware that they were practically drooling. This happened every year. The ball in 1875 took it to the next level.

The horrible winter, combined with the preceding two and a half weeks of May sunshine, created virulent spring fever, emotions heating up, expectations high, patience thin. Perhaps that explains why people became disoriented when Ariana De Vries, just turned seventeen, was introduced. She started a riot. Not on the outside, where polite society almost never shows what is going on inside. Indeed, there was no discernible reaction to Ariana as she stepped forward to do her curtsy for the Honorable William Gaston, governor of Massachusetts. If anything, she got less applause than some of the other girls, particularly from other women. But if there were an instrument that could measure seismic vibrations inside the mind, this moment was off the scale. Granted that the winter had been so awful that a frog might have looked like an angel and stoked up the hormones. But Ariana's impact can be best understood in simple terms. Not only did she not look like a frog; she was the most beautiful debutante in this or any other year. She was the most beautiful woman anyone in the ballroom had ever seen.

So, it is not surprising that Eric Lowell, the youngest Lowell in his clan, nineteen, going on twenty, fell into a swoon the instant he saw her. *Swoon* used to be employed to describe a woman's reaction to a powerful man, a hunk, as they would say today. But in truth, Ariana was having that effect on men and women alike. She shared her mother Belize's French features, but there was also another element, more mysterious, more difficult to pinpoint. Was it Dutch? Flemish? Swiss blood that she carried in her veins alongside the French? Was it her hair? Her lips? Perhaps it was the slight flaw, which saves the truly beautiful from banality, a tiny scar above her right eyebrow, the result of a teacup used as a missile by Ariana's older sister when she was four.

Her skin was as smooth as silk, but moist, like morning dew on a flower. It made her luminescent. She was heart-stopping, show stopping. The moment she appeared, everything else stopped. Simply stopped. There is no other way to describe it. A hush, an instinctive simultaneous gasp from everyone there, a collective sigh, the silent sound of psyches being thrown into disarray, rearranged without a prior plan. Not just Eric's but every eye was drawn to her like a magnet. She dared the shy, she emboldened the brazen to take a longer look.

Ariana's beauty was not the only factor setting the ballroom on fire. It was her lineage. Women who were jealous of her, especially those who had never liked her mother, brought up all of the usual rumors about the identity of her true father. It wasn't just them. Ariana's father, Ernest, and his family had all along treated the rumors as probable. She was rejected by almost all the De Vries family, her father's father, mother, his sisters, though not his brothers. Family members couldn't mask their contempt. Fine, she was likely to look like her mother. But they knew De Vries from non–De Vries, and Ariana wasn't one of them. Not a single one of her features matched those of anyone they knew or could remember. No one dared utter Vincent Van Doren's name. Ernest's livelihood depended on silence, and they could not be sure. But Ernest's dependency on him to maintain his job added to their anger.

All of this was hard on Ariana. Belize herself had been here before. Many times, Belize told her daughter to ignore their coldness, but Ariana was unable to do so. Compared to her two sisters she suffered from the unremitting distance that her father seemed to reserve for her, and her alone. It made Ariana shy around boys and men.

It wasn't only that she might have been the by-product of sin. Ariana was the daughter of a hotel employee, not a member of society. When her mother, Belize, first arrived in Boston, she had similar problems with the upper crust. She didn't care for them, and they especially didn't care for her, since they saw her as Van Doren's attempt to impress them. Eventually, she won most of them over, but Ariana's invitation to the ball aroused their animosity all over again. For there was little they could do. As invited guests, courtesy was required. A few considered not attending the ball. They felt Van Doren was pushing his luck. Most came, however, because they wouldn't miss the Cotillion Ball, one of the best evenings of the year.

"Crazy." That was the verdict of Mrs. Cabot when she told the story twenty years later.

"Tense. Very tense," added Mrs. Holcomb.

Intended or not, Ariana's invitation was a further assault on the Brahmins' world. First a trickle, now the flood. The upstarts already had more money and nicer homes. Their most obnoxious characteristic, their manners, was not half as important as the real issue—their unwillingness to bow to the upper crust. And now one of them had found a way to get invited to the ball. One of them was to be welcomed as a debutante.

"What is next?" Mrs. Elliot whispered to Mrs. Smith. "Are the janitors going to bring their daughters?"

"Are the maids?" piped in Mrs. Smith.

They were not prepared for the final blow. When Ariana stepped out to be introduced to society, it made each of their daughters ordinary. Their night, the night that should have been the grandest of their daughters' childhood, was being spoiled by a hotelkeeper's daughter.

They had their moments. At one point, for just an instant, Arianna tripped on her high heels and almost fell down. The relief that passed through the room was palpable. But unfortunately for them, Ariana's recovery was quick. She was soon comfortably smiling as she swayed to the music.

In the middle of it all sat luftmensch Mr. Henry James. After a lifetime of wandering all over the world seeking God, and the truth, he had found it among the Boston Brahmins, as a resident wise man and philosopher. His beliefs in *being* rather than *doing,* in fellowship resulting from not having to compete, finding God in nature and other people—these sat well with those who resided at the top of society and, like him, didn't have to work. His belief in nature was best experienced by city folk. His nasty competitive side was limited to his family, including his increasingly successful sons. He rarely hesitated to embarrass them with his harangues. Unfortunately for his usual allies, ladies from Boston's finest families, he had nothing to say. He was all man. He was enchanted as much as anyone by Ariana's appearance.

Arianna's beauty was leaving wounds. Mrs. Sergot felt it in her bowels. She took leave for a longish retreat to the powder room. Mrs. Harrison noticed that the muscles in her neck were pinching again. She might have to make a trip to the spa to get those knots out. Dame Gayle Tyler had the beginnings of a headache (one that lasted two days), and Mrs. Nancy Tuttle noticed that she could not quite catch her breath. There were other casualties, not all trivial, but they can't be proven. Mrs. Vigor insisted until she died that her cancer had sprung on her the morning after the ball. For years after, Mrs. Oliver Crompole claimed that the ball had made her daughter go insane, her very pretty daughter, the one everyone expected to be crowned that night as the princess of her generation.

Overbreeding had made them helpless before Ariana's onslaught. The only defense that any of the women could muster was to whisper, gossip, cast glaring looks at her that they tried not to make obvious but that kept breaking through their usually well-exercised smiles. You could feel the tension rising.

A growing collective desire to see Ariana have her comeuppance, a moment capable of ending her spell, gave them hope. For until the actual end of the evening, many possibilities could still rescue their equanimity. Mrs. Turpin, well known for her uncanny bluntness, had a comforting private fantasy that would have done the job: Ariana vomiting over her beautiful gown. That, she felt, would be an excellent solution to the evening. Mrs. Rather's thoughts turned to God. Surely, he would not allow a bastard child to tempt good Christians with worldly indulgences. There were many comforting thoughts throughout the room. However, even as the evening got worse and worse for those suffering from her appearance, one thing remained constant: No one could take his or her eyes off of Ariana.

Eric wished he could approach Ariana like a Latin lover, simply walk over, stick out his chest, and begin from there. One night the previous summer, he and three of his friends had sneaked out, gone to Spanish Town, and saw the way the men approached women.

Ariana had exposed their big talk as a pipe dream. You are who you are. Eric was becoming desperate. She had moved and he was no longer able to get a good look at her from across the room. He would have to act, but he didn't want her to know that he had moved closer. So, he stayed where he was, despite the fact that, more than anything, he needed to look and look and look and look. He wanted to drink her in with his eyes.

If from time to time in his life so far Eric had recognized a vague, uncomfortable feeling that something was missing, now he felt bereft, powerless, broken without it. His grandfather had told him it was his rib. Adam had bestowed that feeling on all men. Now suddenly, Eric needed his rib back. He was broken without it. He needed to know if she would belong to him. And the best he could do was try to get a better look. Then another look and another. Only propriety, not to mention pride, demanded that he could not buzz, could not let his mouth drop and simply stare. The strength of his desire was pushing him to do exactly that. So early in the night, Eric turned to his best defense, the same thing everyone else was doing. He ignored her, or tried to act like he was doing that.

Not only Eric was struck. Mrs. Sergot, Mrs. Harrison, Dame Gayle Tyler, Mrs. Argyle Tuttle, Mrs. Vigor, Mrs.

Oliver Crompole, and twenty, maybe thirty others there that night were in a sorry state. For years after that evening, they tried to ignore Ariana. They would not meet her eyes, not act friendly. They made a point of not seeming impressed or favorably influenced by everything and anything Ariana did or said. They couldn't forgive her. They exacted punishment for the pain she had caused them that night, and it was never enough. There was no suitable amount that could even the score.

There are those who can only regain the safe high ground through contempt (for the very things that have struck their fancy). Ariana subsequently suffered more than her share of being on the losing end of one-upmanship. Over and over, she let down her guard; she didn't see it coming, didn't even suspect their motive until it was too late. Eventually, she caught on and did what was necessary. In her final years, those who didn't know her well thought of her as a bitch. Exactly in proportion to her vulnerability in her 20's, her toughness in her 70's was remarkable. However, all of this happened later, as it often does, when not just her, but many other people gain enough time to perfect their best defenses. That night, motivations were early and pure, and thus more poisonous. The disquieting wonder that took hold when she entered the room, the awe dictated what the polite were forced to do that night. After her introduction, only stolen glances were possible.

Eric stole a lot of them. He couldn't help himself. Unlike some of his pals, Eric had thought about falling in love before it happened to him. But he hadn't taken into account just how much love could seize him. He loved the way she walked, loved the way she smiled, loved the way she brought her index finger to brush against her nose when she felt an itch. As she first entered he noticed a small scar above her eyebrow, which strengthened his feelings. He loved the scar.

The more he noticed, the more he loved. Each and every observation intensified his pain. It didn't matter what she did, or what he learned. He was smitten. So were at least twenty other young men who had nearly identical feelings. But it was worse for Eric. He was completely miserable. There was only one answer for what now plagued him—finding out if she loved him. A very straightforward issue, his grandfather would counsel. "You have a question. You get the answer."

Yes or no. No mystery. Nothing to analyze. "What is the big deal?" say believers in mind over matter. Only anyone who has been there, young or old, knows that this question is a form of torture. Love makes you its prisoner. You need the answer. Need it, not want it. You can't sleep without it; you can't think without it. You can't do anything. The question is on your mind constantly. You want to know her. You have to know her. Conventional wisdom is nonsense. It is not better to have loved and lost. Love is dangerous unless it is returned. It can destroy a happy disposition, change a person to long-lasting, sometimes permanent, bitterness. That aspect is democratic. Love has destroyed kings, captains of football teams, cool dudes, and accountants. Some people never venture to the next step, never truly take the chance. Some won't go there again. Not like the first time, when despair visited at the slightest bad news, after the briefest indifferent glance.

Unfortunately for Eric, there was a more serious challenge. One very important suitor, Andrew Holden, age thirty-six, was still unmarried. He had come to Boston to meet with Vincent Van Doren for business. He had heard Boston was the best place to find Van Doren receptive to new introductions. Van Doren, now seventy-seven years old, was impressed with the young man's grit. He saw a bit of himself in him. He immediately thought Ariana would make a wonderful match. If he could cement the deal with Ariana, it would be good for her, good for Holden, and good for the business between them. He had Ariana and her parents, Belize and Ernest De Vries, to lunch with Mr. Holden. It didn't take long for Van Doren to notice Holden's interest. Indeed, after their lunch, Andrew visited a jeweler and bought a very fine sapphire and diamond brooch to present to Ariana that evening, with the hope that the ball might go as he expected.

Ariana was not immune to the extreme reactions stirring up around her. She herself had been taken aback by her appearance as she caught herself in the hallway mirror before leaving the family suite at the hotel. She stopped and stared for a few moments. It was as if she were looking at another person. She had never been allowed to wear a woman's gown. She had never pulled up her hair quite like that. She could see that she was beautiful. It wasn't conceit, or even self-satisfaction. In fact, what she saw in the mirror made her uneasy. Even before the tension developed at the ball, she instinctively knew that what she was looking at was not quite from the ordinary world. In New England, God's creatures were expected to be ordinary. The devil is more likely to favor perfection. When she began to tremble, she, too, had to look away. She had the kind of beauty that hurts, that makes others hurt themselves, or hurt someone else, or hurt her, beauty that could only bring pain.

Which is ironic; words like *sweet,* or *loving* come to mind to describe Ariana's actual disposition. She was a friendly, nice girl. The young lady who had suddenly appeared in the mirror was anything but the Ariana she herself had known. Well, not completely. Beauty had always received special emphasis in her values. She was taught the usual by her mother—that beauty is only skin-deep, that beauty is superficial and temporary and unimportant. Like her mother, however, she couldn't fool herself. If it was temporary, it was all the more valuable. As long as she could remember, and even tonight, her mother's beauty thrilled her. When Belize got dressed for an occasion, and there were many occasions, she would go into Ariana's room to give her a kiss good night. Ariana would cry out, even at two and three years old, "Oh, Mommy, you look so pretty!"

Perhaps every girl identifies with Cinderella, wonders if one night she will be Cinderella precisely because of her very unprincesslike circumstances. Not just Cinderella. The fairy tales have a common element, a beautiful young woman imprisoned in a tower, or with a spell put upon her so that she remains asleep; the men, too, frogs or beasts that become princes, brought to life by a kiss. Year after year, Ariana prayed and wished and fantasized that someday . . .

someday, maybe, you never know, maybe she could look like her mother. She didn't seriously think it was possible. Until the night of the ball, she had not realized her wish would be granted. She had been plump as a child, pleasant, eager to please, quickly forgettable.

And now suddenly, her past might as well have never happened. One look into the mirror and she instinctively knew her life had been permanently altered. She finally had what she had always wanted. She just hadn't expected that her first emotion, after realizing she had been granted her dream, would be trepidation rather than happiness. She had long wondered—she couldn't wait to know—how it would feel to be a woman. Tonight, the wondering was over. The beginning had arrived. It was like sliding down a sheet of ice, no screaming allowed.

Chapter 7

By the middle of the evening, Eric was in even worse shape. He had been whipped into a lather. Tradition allowed young men to become idiotic, to add a little racing fuel to their veins, Jamaican rum. Their foolishness was part of the evening's entertainment for the older men in attendance. Watching the young men act stupidly restored their place in society, their function. They became indignant, and thus were appreciated as keepers of community standards.

Stirring up Eric's courage made him uncharacteristically wild. Or perhaps it wasn't the fuel. A lot of people that night were changing substantially in very little time, or were about to change. Before tonight, Eric had been comfortable enough. He had had a nice long run at being a boy, teasing, toying with, torturing his buddies for the fun of it. And able to take it when they returned the favor. Puppies do the same thing to each other. Fun fights, nips, chases. He hadn't been in any particular hurry to see that end. It never occurred to him that it would end. But in an instant, in that first look at Ariana, Eric's childhood cocoon, which had always seemed to contain his entire universe, had turned into an empty shell. His puppyhood was over.

Fortunately for Eric, he was a Lowell, which counted for something in Boston. But more important than his breeding, he could count on his youthful cockiness to move him forward, especially reinforced by his introduction to bottled spirits. It was a weird feeling, like he could leap without fear of falling. He didn't know whether he liked the heightened energy or distrusted it. But he and his equally soused friends were making too much noise. For a moment, he attracted the disapproving attention of the sponsor of the ball, Vincent Van Doren. Eric's position in society stopped Van Doren from saying anything. Besides, other than his misgivings about Eric's group, Van Doren was thoroughly enjoying himself.

This was the gala affair he had always wanted, and Ariana was the belle of the ball. At first, her shyness overcame any other instinct. She felt their stares. But then, toward the middle of the evening, after Eric asked her to dance, her transformation was complete. She could see the way Eric looked at her, his eagerness, his alertness to even a spark of interest from her. It freed her. But there was something else. He was sweet.

"Sorry," he mumbled at the beginning of the dance after he stepped on her toe. It was not self-consciousness. It was concern for her toe. But then they got started and he was better, and then better, and then very fine indeed. His natural grace was an essential ingredient, but something else was happening. His body had become an instrument of his worship. He felt the music take over his limbs. The same thing was happening to her. They felt suspended; they felt lightness as the two of them lost themselves in twirls across the floor, in effortless motion, gliding like ice-skaters on the Charles River. She followed him like a woman in love. Her body knew Eric's intention before he did. Neither had a sense of the other's will. They were without awareness of will.

But when the dance finished, their bond immediately dissolved. He stiffened as they came off the floor. She waved to one of the men she had danced with earlier, and that seemed to totally end what they had. He became strangely formal and polite. Perhaps he didn't know what to say, what to do next. Perhaps his nerves simply failed. Later, she would go over these things in fine detail. He awkwardly thanked her for the dance, and then he left, to get lost among his friends, who were giving him a hale and hearty salute with their raised glasses of rum.

Ariana asked herself what she had done that might explain losing him, but she couldn't come up with an explanation. A careful observer could see that she had done nothing, but when Ariana now and again looked Eric's way, she wasn't able to capture even a flicker of interest. He had become indistinguishable from everyone else, meaning that, like almost every young man there that night, he was doing his best not to let on how much he wanted to stare and study her. So Ariana's glimpses of Eric went unnoticed. Once or twice, she thought she caught him looking differently her way. A few times, Eric also thought he saw interest on her part. But that is the nature of such episodes. Lovers are invariably out of phase. Eric, in particular, took what he thought was her indifference hard. He was becoming increasingly pessimistic about his chances, especially because almost every time he looked her way, she seemed to be enjoying herself. Her partner for the last three dances was Andrew Holden, who had no difficulty asking her again and again for the next dance. And she refused none of his advances.

As the evening drew closer to an end, Eric felt pathetic. What had gone wrong? As they always did for one another, his friends assured him that it would all turn out okay. But tonight, the usual fibs weren't working. Then, as the music began for what he thought might be the last dance, he caught a look from Ariana. Or he thought he did. He wasn't sure if he read it correctly, but now frantic, he was willing to take his chances. He walked right over to her in the middle of the ballroom. She had already moved to the middle of the ballroom with Holden. Eric cut in front. He offered his hand. She took it and the two of them danced off, leaving Holden standing alone like a fool. Van Doren caught that moment. He was not happy about it. Holden was a man like himself, self-made. He didn't know about Lowell.

Because it was a warm evening, along the entire length of the ballroom, the French doors were left open to the veranda so that dancers could cool off under the stars. That night, they expected the usual, Boston's bracing sea air. But the air was thick with the fragrance of magnolia, and it cast a spell. The magnolia tree in the courtyard had been placed there under the direction and inspiration of Henry McBride, from Savannah, Georgia. It had been brought, or, more accurately, bought, north in 1851 from the Jefferson

Rogers estate, where Van Doren had stayed for a weekend, and decided there, on the spot, to bring a bit of the South to Boston. He thought that would make Belize happy, which it did. Van Doren wasn't invited back to the Rogers estate, but he felt he had gotten the better of the deal.

In Boston, magnolia blossoms normally appear, if at all, very early in the spring. They are easily destroyed by a nighttime frost. That year, the appearance of the buds and the opening of the blossoms were greatly delayed by the frigid early spring. When they finally bloomed the day of the ball, the tree was in all its glory. After their dance, Eric and Ariana leaned on the iron railing, wondering about the stars. They were both looking beyond, looking where they might go together. She lived at the hotel. She knew the garden's secrets.

Beyond the veranda courtyard, and behind the Japanese maple, a gate invites the curious to follow a spiral path down to Belize's rose garden. The scent pulls you forward long before your eyes are dazzled by its beauty. To this very day, it is still lit by gas lanterns. They produce a small flame that barely penetrates the darkness, a faintness of light that has been repeatedly useful, generation after generation, to couples in search of privacy. The lanterns, purchased by Van Doren himself in Paris, cast a strange glow, especially on moonlit evenings. Belize had once brought Ariana here on just such a night. Her roses invite the eyes to their satiny wine red petals grayed by the darkness. Here the shadows converge into blackness in the center of each bud. Ariana guided Eric to a bush she had planted with her mother on her fifth birthday. Its most enticing characteristic was that some years it began to bloom in mid-May. This night, in the velvety moonlight, a perfect blossom waited. Eric plucked it and presented it to her in the darkness. She slowly, gently pulled the slightly moist flower across her cheeks until she brought it to her nostrils. The sounds of the orchestra drifted in and out of their attention.

He stood very close behind her, humming almost in a whisper. Eric put his arms around her waist. They instinctively moved to the music. Ariana closed her eyes and imagined the two of them on their wedding day as they left the church, first smiling, then grinning. She couldn't remember when she had last grinned. Her mother's happy eyes met hers at that moment. The image flashed into her mind and was gone as quickly.

"What are you thinking?"

"Nothing," she replied.

She took his hand and led him out of the rose garden, down a path, to the pond covered with lily pads. Vincent had built it at Belize's request. When it was finished, they had walked there alone. Only once, but that was enough.

Eric and Ariana crossed a footbridge to an island with a gazebo. At the time Vincent brought it from Atlanta, no one had ever seen anything like it. In the future, this spot would be known as Ariana's Kiss. In the 1940s, generations of young ladies experienced their first kiss here, often after the prom, a kiss they still could recall when they became grandmothers. Later, the spot went out of style, and the story was forgotten. Eventually, the sign marking the spot came down and wasn't replaced, as no one could remember or explain why there was a sign, or who Ariana was, and what the kiss was about. Everyone agreed the whole thing was dumb anyway, at least until it was rediscovered by a retro-look designer, hired by management to spruce up the place.

This was the spot where Eric kissed Ariana. Her first kiss. His first love. In later reveries, which remained with Ariana until her last breath, she could remember the distant sound of the orchestra. It had mixed with the melodies and rhythms of cicadas. She could remember the taste of his lips. The way she had moaned ever so slightly, without embarrassment, the touch of his tongue on her scar, the way she'd trembled. She'd been completely his prisoner. Anything he'd asked, she would have given. She'd wanted to be with him forever.

The music stopped. They were both suddenly aware of time. People would start to wonder. Her mother had not seen her leave. They planned where they would meet the next day. He took off his ring and gave it to her. She slipped it on, caressing it with her other hand. Eric kissed the ring on her hand.

Stories about the Clarkson continued long after Van Doren and Ariana were gone. The old-timers, who, to this day, still frequent Sunday lunch in the main dining room, repeat the tales again and again. By far the most talked-about part of the Clarkson's history is the spot where, as you enter the ballroom from the veranda via the door at the far right, there is a faded but still visible stain where blood soaked into the floor. It's Eric Lowell's blood. Who killed him is unclear. The record is somewhere, but no one is curious enough or able to go through the dust to find out what actually happened.

One story has it that it was one of Holden's men. Holden had approached Ariana as she and Eric returned. She rebuffed him, which made him all the more insistent. Eric, perhaps influenced by the booze, or by his passion, shoved him hard. Too hard. Holden tripped and went down. Holden reached in his pocket, and in response, Eric reached in his pocket, and almost immediately he had a knife in his hand. Probably Eric showed it to Holden to tell him to back off. But Holden was also drunk, and he got up and came right at Eric. Eric raised his hand with the knife. Then Holden's men seemed to appear from out of nowhere. A shot rang out.

Or so one version of the story goes. Another version has it that the perpetrator was a Van Doren employee. Another that they scuffled and it was an accident. Whatever the case, whether the perpetrator was properly punished has long since become irrelevant.

Ariana held Eric in her arms. He was conscious for at least five minutes. She couldn't make out what he was saying. Then, silence. She knew it was over, but, at the same time, she didn't know. With his head in her lap, she started to rock. Her legs pulsed up and down. She sobbed as her hips moved, shaking him, shaking him, waking him, insisting, encouraging, then, finally, gently releasing him to sleep.

He remained motionless. A doctor appeared from among the guests. He moved Ariana away and pronounced Eric dead. Belize arrived and held her daughter tightly, very tightly, trying to squeeze her love into her. At first, Ariana was lifeless, but then she began to tremble. So Belize held her even more tightly until she stopped, and then started to rock her. They were both covered with Eric's blood. It was everywhere, and remnants of it are still there today. An artistic historical map describing the incident is framed and hangs near the door in question.

After Eric's death, not much was heard about Ariana for over a decade. She lived with her parents in the family's suite at the Van Doren Hotel. There are actually two portraits of Ariana in the Clarkson, one of her as a child with the rest of the De Vries children, the other after her retirement from the hotel's management. After Belize died (Ernest De Vries had died a decade earlier), Ariana continued to live in the suite and took over management of the hotel. In truth, Van Doren's son, and later his granddaughters, treated Ariana with patronizing charity, which eventually grew thin. But they never made her leave. It was rumored that this was due to a stipulation in Van Doren's will. Perhaps. Perhaps not. In any case, she remained true to Eric. She never married. There was nowhere else to go, nowhere else she wanted to be. Unlike her mother, she wasn't a social creature. She kept to herself.

Only her employees appreciated her passion and her genius. Only her employees knew that they were working for an inspired taskmaster. Only they loved her. It didn't matter to her that they had heard the rumor that she was Vincent Van Doren's love child. She had come to believe it. Her dedication to the Clarkson was not because of the stipulations in Van Doren's will. It was a monument to that evening, a monument to Eric and her love. For at least thirty years, employees knew that they worked on sacred ground. Really until the middle of the 1960s, when the world of privilege, of debutantes, and of magnolia was mocked as totally uncool.

But even the sixties didn't completely end it. It had been a long time since there were grand balls. But the workers at the hotel treated the room with respect. Even the Ecuadorians, who came to work there in the late nineties and did not speak English, knew. Even the sarcastic workers, many generations of them, despite the jokes that were inevitable, also treated the ballroom with a kind of love that they could not explain. But then, anything that Belize had given birth to had that effect. It continues to the present day.

But they are also being influenced by Ariana, who improved upon her mother's conception. Perhaps the story of Ariana and Eric is true, perhaps not. It is certainly true that, as was the case with her suspected father, hard work defined Ariana's soul, and passion, which she could not control and to which she gave free rein.